THE AMAZING

ADVENTURES OF

HARRY MOON

OPERATION BIG TOP

by

Mark Andrew Poe

with Barry Napier

Illustrations by Christina Weidman

rabbit publishers

Operation Big Top (The Amazing Adventures of Harry Moon)
by Mark Andrew Poe
with Barry Napier
© Copyright 2017 by Mark Andrew Poe. All rights reserved.

Rabbit Publishers
1624 W. Northwest Highway
Arlington Heights, IL 60004

Illustrations by Christina Weidman
Interior Design by Lewis Design & Marketing
Creative Consultants: David Kirkpatrick, Thom Black, and Paul Lewis

ISBN: 978-1-943785-32-2

10 9 8 7 6 5 4 3 2 1

1. Fiction - Action and Adventure 2. Children's Fiction
First Edition
Printed in U.S.A.

"From time to time,
everyone needs a little help."

~ *Rabbit*

TABLE OF CONTENTS

PROLOGUE

Halloween visited the little town of Sleepy Hollow and never left.

Many moons ago, a sly and evil mayor found the powers of darkness helpful in building Sleepy Hollow into "Spooky Town," one of the country's most celebrated attractions. Now, years later, a young eighth grade magician, Harry Moon, is chosen by the powers of light to do battle against the mayor and his evil consorts.

Welcome to *The Amazing Adventures of Harry Moon*. Darkness may have found a home in Sleepy Hollow, but if young Harry has anything to say about it, darkness will not be staying.

FAMILY, FRIENDS & FOES

Harry Moon

Harry is the thirteen-year-old hero of Sleepy Hollow. He is a gifted magician who is learning to use his abilities and understand what it means to possess the real magic.

An unlikely hero, Harry is shorter than his classmates and has a shock of inky, black hair. He loves his family and his town. Along with his friend Rabbit, Harry is determined to bring Sleepy Hollow back to its true and wholesome glory.

Rabbit

Now you see him. Now you don't. Rabbit is Harry Moon's friend. Some see him. Most can't.

Rabbit is a large, black-and-white, lop-eared, Harlequin rabbit. As Harry has discovered, having a friend like Rabbit has its consequences. Never stingy with advice and counsel, Rabbit always has Harry's back as Harry battles the evil that has overtaken Sleepy Hollow.

Honey Moon

She's a ten-year-old, sassy spitfire. And she's Harry's little sister. Honey likes to say she goes where she is needed, and sometimes this takes her into the path of danger.

Honey never gives in and never gives up when it comes to righting a wrong. Honey always looks out for her friends. Honey does not like that her town has been plunged into a state of eternal Halloween and is even afraid of the evil she feels lurking all around. But if Honey has anything to say about it, evil will not be sticking around.

Samson Dupree

Samson is the enigmatic owner of the Sleepy Hollow Magic Shoppe. He is Harry's mentor and friend. When needed, Samson teaches Harry new tricks and helps him understand his gift of magic.

Samson arranged for Rabbit to become Harry's sidekick and friend. Samson is a timeless, eccentric man who wears purple robes, red slippers, and a gold crown. Sometimes, Samson shows up in mysterious ways. He even appeared to Harry's mother shortly after Harry's birth.

Mary Moon

Strong, fair, and spiritual, Mary Moon is Harry and Honey's mother. She is also mother to two-year-old Harvest. Mary is married to John Moon.

Mary is learning to understand Harry and his destiny. So far, she is doing a good job letting Harry and Honey fight life's battles. She's grateful that Rabbit has come alongside to support and counsel her. But like all moms, Mary often finds it difficult to let her children walk their own paths. Mary is a nurse at Sleepy Hollow Hospital.

John Moon

John is the dad. He's a bit of a nerd. He works as an IT professional, and sometimes he thinks he would love it if his children followed in his footsteps. But he respects that Harry, Honey, and possibly Harvest will need to go their own way. John owns a classic sports car he calls Emma.

Titus Kligore

Titus is the mayor's son. He is a bully of the first degree but also quite conflicted when it comes to Harry. The two have managed to forge a tentative friendship, although Titus will assert his bully strength on Harry from time to time.

Titus is big. He towers over Harry. But in a kind of David vs. Goliath way, Harry has learned which tools are best to counteract Titus's assaults while most of the Sleepy Hollow kids fear him. Titus would probably rather not be a bully, but with a dad like Maximus Kligore, he feels trapped in the role.

Maximus Kligore

The epitome of evil, nastiness, and greed, Maximus Kligore is the mayor of Sleepy Hollow. To bring in the cash, Maximus turned the town into the nightmarish, Halloween attraction it is today.

He commissions the evil-tinged celebrations in town. Maximus is planning to take Sleepy Hollow with him to Hell. But will he? He knows Harry Moon is a threat to his dastardly ways, but try as he might, he has yet to rid himself of Harry's meddling.

Kligore lives on Folly Farm and owns most of the town, including the town newspaper.

V

THE CARNIVAL
COMES TO TOWN

For a town where it is always Halloween
night, any change can be a welcome one.
The slightest shift in the normal schedule
of things can cause excitement and wonder in
children and grown-ups alike. This was exactly
what happened when the northeast corner
of Sleepy Hollow started to smell like sweet
things.

Not just sweet things but sticky sweet things. Of vanilla syrup and sugar dustings and the epic aromas of funnel cakes. Then came the whiff of roasting peanuts. After that, there was the waft of hot-buttered popcorn. With all the whiffs and wafts of those abounding favors, was it any wonder that a kid could not get anything done?

In Sleepy Hollow, Massachusetts, the circus had come to town. And not just any circus. This was Clive Cantaloni's Carnival and Magic Show.

As opening day approached, the kids in town grew more and more excited. It was all anyone talked about in school, especially when the sounds of elephants and lions started to fill the night air, taking the place of the usual crickets and owls.

But of all of the town's residents, there was no one more excited than Harry Moon. As a talented magician always looking to perfect his craft, Harry could not wait to see the show. But more than that, he could not wait to meet Clive Cantaloni. The way Harry figured it, if he could impress Mr. Cantaloni, he might just be able to earn a spot in the ring of Clive Cantaloni's Carnival and Magic Show.

But until that moment came, Harry, like all of the other kids in town, could only wait and continue to smell the sticky, dizzying magic that only a carnival could create.

"Here it is!"

3

Harry Moon slapped a poster down on the Moons' dining room table. Plop! It was a poster he had gotten from school. The poster was brightly colored and showed a very proud-looking man sitting on the back of an elephant. The elephant was wearing a tutu, surrounded by lions, tigers, flaming hoops, joyful clowns, and an array of fried food floating like ghosts. At the top of the poster, perfectly curved around the elephant's backside, were the words **Clive Cantaloni's Carnival and Magic Show!**

"Yes, that's nice dear," Mary Moon said. "We're all very excited about Mr. Cantaloni's carnival. "Now could you kindly remove that poster from my lasagna?"

"Sorry," Harry said. He removed the poster

from the table but still held it up. "I was wondering if maybe you'd let me meet with him."

"With Mr. Cantaloni?" John Moon asked.

"Yes," Harry answered. "I want to see if he'd let me do magic at the carnival."

Mary Moon smiled. "That's a very lofty goal," Harry's mom replied. "I think it would be great for you—and that you could nail it. I think it's a wonderful idea."

"Well, I'm not going to that stinky, old carnival," Honey Moon said. She was Harry's younger sister and rarely had issues with sharing what was on her mind.

"Why not?" Harry asked, shocked.

"The lions and tigers on that poster may look like they're having a great time, but carnivals and people that work for circuses keep those poor animals in cages!"

Harry rolled his eyes. "But they're treated with kindness," he said. He was pretty sure this was true. Truth be told, he also had issues with those awesome, majestic animals being locked up. But he also knew that it was all part of the show.

"Would you like it if Mom and Dad made *you* stay in a cage all day?" Honey asked.

"Well, no . . . but—"

"But nothing," Honey snapped. "It's not right, and I plan on doing something about it!

"Like what?" Mary Moon asked.

"I don't know," Honey said. "But I'll think of something!"

The dinner table fell quiet for a moment. The only noise came from little Harvest, sitting in his high chair, slapping two lasagna noodles together.

"So would it be okay if I went by the

fairgrounds tomorrow to meet him?" Harry asked. "The carnival doesn't even start until Saturday afternoon. If I can talk to him tomorrow, I might have just enough time to convince him to let me have a spot."

He watched as his parents shared a look across the table. Harry sometimes wondered if married people could communicate telepathically—using only their minds. It sure seemed like his parents were able to do it every now and then.

With a shrug, Mary Moon finally answered. "I think that would be okay," she said. "Why not swing by there tomorrow after school? But Harry . . . you have to understand. Mr. Cantaloni is a professional. No matter how talented you are, you can't be upset if he doesn't take you on."

"That's right," John Moon said. "There's a very good chance that he already has a very specific schedule. He could *love* you but just not be able to work you in."

"I know," Harry said, poking at his lasagna. And while he *did* know this, there was a spark of excitement that whispered to him: *You're a perfect fit. Of course, he'll want you!*

"Don't get too excited," Honey said. "If I have my way, I'm going to figure out how to shut that mean, old circus down!"

Harry and Honey stared each other down over the table. While they had the usual sibling spats, they usually got along fairly well. But every now and then a hot topic issue like this one would get them riled up.

A cheerful shout from Harvest broke the awkward silence. He was pointing at the poster which was now sitting beside Harry.

"Lion!" Harvest said, pointing with one of his noodles. He contorted his face into the powerful king of the jungle. "Roar!" he cried.

The tension between Harry and Honey was broken. Everyone at the table started laughing, all except for Harvest. He continued to roar at

the poster. Clive Cantaloni looked out at the Moon family from his red saddle on the back of his elephant. He was an imposing man with rough features. As powerful as he was, Clive Cantaloni appeared to be laughing, too.

10

AUDITION TIME

When the final bell rang at Sleepy Hollow Middle School the following day, Harry couldn't get out of the building fast enough. He was so excited to get to the fairgrounds that he even bailed out of school before meeting up with Declan, Bailey, and Hao like he did every day. As he dashed away from the entrance stairs and jumped onto his bike, he got a few puzzled glances from his schoolmates, but he barely noticed.

As he grew closer to the center of town, he slowed a bit to watch out for afternoon traffic. He peddled his way through Magic Row, past the Sleepy Hollow Pumpkin Patch, and kept heading north. Ahead of him, he could see those huge tent tops, calling out to him like a lighthouse. Harry couldn't remember the last time he had been this excited or happy.

In fact, he was so anxious to get to Clive Cantaloni's fairgrounds that he barely even noticed when he passed by Folly Farm, the estate that held the We Drive by Night headquarters. It was also the home of Mayor Maximus Kligore—a man he could easily call his arch nemesis.

Harry barely saw any of this. His eyes were fixed on the big top tents that were starting to loom larger as he came to the northwest edge of town. As he pumped his bike hard on Witch Broom Road to Herman Melville Field, he came to a large fence that had been erected around the tent grounds.

A single entrance, an iron gate, stood at the dirt road off of Witch Broom leading into the

fairgrounds. Over the gate, a large arched sign bore a cartoon of Clive Cantaloni's face.

His white hair was thick and long as a lion's mane. Beneath bushy, white eyebrows, his piercing, brown eyes stared out from his head, embodying the mysterious excitement of the world of the big top. Huge letters read **Welcome to Clive Cantaloni's Carnival and Magic Show!**

Harry looked at the large, iron entrance and saw that it was not latched to the post. He supposed there had been trucks going in and out of the site all day so leaving it locked would have been a huge waste of time. He spent only a moment wondering if what he was about to do would be considered trespassing. He figured so long as the place wasn't locked, he should be in the clear. After jumping from his bike, he leaned it against the fence.

13

Slipping through the opening betwee the gate and the post, he stepped onto the tented grounds.

He was sure it was only his imagination, but all of the smells that had wafted for so long from Herman Melville Field seemed stronger now that he was on the other side of the gate. There were all those sticky smells of candied apples, cotton candy, and funnel cakes.

He found this odd because he wasn't sure why they would be cooking such stuff yet. The carnival wouldn't be officially open for business until tomorrow afternoon. But there were numerous workers walking back and forth through the fairgrounds, and he thought, *they all needed to eat! What a great life working for the circus. Funnel cakes for breakfast, lunch, and dinner!*

Some of the workers, dressed in bright red, orange, and blue zip-up uniforms, carried smaller tents that had yet to be put up. Others constructed booths for the carnival games. Harry saw the Test Your Strength Machine, Dunk a Duck, Ring Toss, and Rocket Blast games. He imagined kids crowding around them tomorrow. He watched as two men walked around one of the rides—a steel contraption with several long metal arms called the Octopus—checking the buckles and latches on the doors.

Somewhere nearby, Harry heard a large cat roar. Somewhere else, someone was playing calliope music. Without the crowd of the carnival around to drown it out, the music sounded cheerful but very, very loud.

15

Looking around in amazement, Harry Moon nearly walked right into the tall clown that was walking in front of him. Seeing the clown at the last minute, Harry stopped quickly. He peered up and finally saw his brightly colored face ten feet over his head. It took Harry a while to figure it out, but he was certain the clown was walking on stilts.

"So sorry," Harry said. "Excuse me!"

16

"No worries," the clown replied from far above Harry's head. "You know, the carnival doesn't open until tomorrow afternoon."

"I know," Harry said. "I was hoping to speak with Mr. Cantaloni."

"Oh! I think he's in the bigger tent. The red one. He's pretty busy, though. I don't know if he's open to visitors right now. But hey, it never hurts to try, right?"

"Right," Harry replied. The clown nodded, gave a squeak of his big, rubber nose, and walked on. Harry watched him pass, amazed at how someone could walk so easily on stilts.

AUDITION TIME

Harry headed for the three tents at the center of the fairgrounds. The largest tent was bright red and stood at least one hundred feet tall. He could hear banging and clanging, laughter and shouts, and roars and all kinds of sounds coming from within the tent.

Through the flaps of the tent, Harry walked inside. He froze for a moment. Although it was empty, Harry thought the inside of the tent looked awesome. It looked much taller than it did from the outside. He observed the bleachers. He quickly calculated that a thousand or so people could fit in here easily.

A thousand people, Harry Moon thought. *I could be performing in front of a thousand people!* The most Harry had ever performed in front of was about half that in the auditorium for the school talent show. Of course, he had millions of hits from his YouTube videos, but this was the *largest live audience he had ever had! Well, if he could actually get into the circus ring.*

Out in the center of the tent, on a large, ring-shaped floor, Harry saw a few people walking back and forth. They were setting up a small wall between the tent floor and the bleachers. Overhead, he saw a tightrope. A woman rehearsed.

In the center of it all, setting up what looked like some sort of stand or platform, was a tall and wide man dressed in an orange suit. He was smoking a cigar. His white, lion mane of hair was as rich and long as the drawings Harry had seen of him on the posters.

18

It was Clive Cantaloni. His cigar sent small clouds of smoke into the air. Harry grinned widely when he saw each little puff of smoke curling itself into the smoky shape of a circus animal. Rising into the air was a lion. Then a monkey. Then a tiger. Finally, a parrot.

Harry breathed deeply. It took all the gumption Harry had to walk down to the ring and speak to him.

"Mr. Cantaloni?" Harry said.

The great man in the orange suit turned. His large, brown eyes grew small at the sight of Harry. They regarded the intruder with caution. "Hey kid, how did you get in here?" Clive Cantaloni grunted. His voice was as huge as his figure, as gruff as any animal.

"The gate was unlocked," Harry said.

"Oh, I see," Mr. Cantaloni replied. He drew another puff on his cigar. This time an elephant rose into the air. "And I suppose you want some sort of special sneak preview, is that it?"

"Oh, no, sir," Harry said. Suddenly, Harry Moon found it hard to speak in front of the monumental man.

"Then what is it? Come on, speak up, boy. I'm very busy today."

"Well, I was wondering if you had any room in the schedule for another act. I'm a magician, and I thought I could—"

"A magician, eh?" Mr. Cantaloni asked, looking Harry over.

"Yes, sir."

19

"Can you disappear on command?"

"No, sir."

"Can you make a member of the audience disappear on cue?"

"Um . . . not always, sir."

"Hmm. What *can* you do?"

20

"Lots of things," Harry said. "I've done tons of magic shows at birthday parties. I can make a rabbit talk. He's as high as my waist, but I can pull him out of my small top hat and . . ."

"Pull it out of your hat?" Mr. Cantaloni laughed. "Are you kidding me, son? No one wants to see that boring, old stuff anymore. And you know . . . even if you were a great magician, I just can't let *anyone* on my stage. If I let one person on, then everyone will be asking for favors."

"Yes sir, I understand," Harry said. "But I think if you give me a chance, you'd see that I . . ."

"Look, kid, I'm sure you're a great magician

to your parents and friends. But this is the big time. Not just anyone can take the stage at Clive Cantaloni's Magic Show. I've got a parrot that can shuffle a deck of cards. There's a monkey that can saw another monkey in half. I've got a woman that can take her head off, set it on the other side of the stage, and her head will drink a glass of water. This is big time showtime, my boy! I don't have room for pulling bunnies out of hats!"

Harry Moon sensed the invisible wall that Clive Cantaloni had built around him. No magic on earth could smash a wall like that. For Harry, he knew that his first impression was his last impression . . . at least, for now. This was not the time for Harry.

Harry looked down to the ground. "Yes, sir. I get it. Goodbye, and thank you for your time."

Harry started walking away, back toward the exit flaps of the tent. He had made it only a few steps when Mr. Cantaloni called out to him. "Hey, kid!"

"Yes?" Harry said, hope blooming in his

heart.

"Be sure to come by Saturday. And bring all of your friends!"

Harry only nodded as he turned away again. He left the tent. He walked through the fairgrounds. Now, with his hopes dashed, the place didn't seem quite so magical. Even the clown walking on his stilts had grown dim in his eyes.

22

With his head hung low, Harry headed back for the main gate.

But before he made it back to Witch Broom Road that would lead him back into Sleepy Hollow, Harry heard a little girl weeping.

PART OF THE ACT

The crying was coming from behind one of the three trucks parked along the far left side of the fairgrounds. Never one to turn away from someone in need of cheering up, Harry started walking toward the trucks. It was then that he realized that one of the trucks had a huge cage on the back of it.

The sobbing sound was coming to a stop, but Harry still heard a few sniffles. He followed it around to the side of the truck and saw not just a little girl but a boy as well. The girl looked to be about the same age as Honey, nine or so. The boy was a little older but still younger than Harry. They were opening a sack of bone meal pellets for the animal's next meal.

When they saw Harry, the kids' expressions changed. They stopped what they were doing. The boy's face grew wolfish as if in defense or aggression, wanting to protect the girl and

24

himself against the intruder, Harry Moon. The little girl's expression became timid, frightened. But they appeared weak and needy, perhaps even lost.

"Don't be afraid," Harry said softly. Despite the gentleness in Harry's voice, the little girl recoiled. Her blonde hair was dirty and unbrushed. The boy's face was smudged with dust. His hair was dirty too. It stood up as if it had something sticky in it. They both looked in need of a bath, and their clothes were equally filthy. "I didn't mean to scare you," Harry said. "I just heard you crying and wanted to make sure you were okay."

25

As Harry spoke, the boy seemed to retreat from his wolfish look. A stoic calm came over his face.

"Are you okay?" Harry asked.

"Yeah, we're fine," the boy said quickly. Harry noticed the boy taking the little girl's hand.

Harry stood for a moment in front of the

boy and girl and then turned to leave them alone. It was clear that he was making them uncomfortable. But just as he was about to depart, Harry sensed a presence standing directly behind him. It was a mysterious presence, but one to whom he was accustomed. The breath on his neck made him shiver at the most important times in Harry Moon's life.

Harry could see Rabbit out of the corner of his eye. Having Rabbit there made the situation seem a little less worrisome.

"Maybe something's not quite right here," Rabbit whispered in Harry's ear.

Hmm, Harry thought. He looked back at the girl and boy, trying to figure out what it might be. *Why were they opening the bone meal sack? Were they truly going to feed the animals? Or were they going to feed themselves? It was probably easier to get to bone meal than to the funnel cakes.* While they tried to hide and not express any emotion, Harry could sense how miserable the two children were.

"Are you hurt?" Harry asked. The girl, in particular, looked troubled.

"No, we're not hurt," the boy said.

"Well . . . do you work here?" Harry asked.

"Yes, we work here," the boy said. "With the carnival."

"Oh," Harry asked. It made a weird sort of sense. *Perhaps, they were this dirty because they had been working for Mr. Cantaloni all day.* But that didn't quite fit. He'd seen clowns and carnival barkers, and they had all been dressed in bright, carnival colors. Even the guys that had been working on the Octopus had been wearing bright zip-up maintenance uniforms. But these two kids were dressed in dingy, battered T-shirts and jeans.

21

Also, everyone else who was working here seemed to be in a very good mood—just as excited as the kids in town were to come see the carnival. But these two kids did not look happy at all. They were frightened.

"What do you do here?" Harry asked.

"We feed the animals. And we're super busy," the boy said. "Now, will you please let us go about our work?"

Harry still felt Rabbit there with him. Rabbit would not have shown up if there wasn't something worth investigating. But at the same time, Harry could tell when he was not wanted. He'd already been shot down by Clive Cantaloni. He sure wasn't going to stick around to be sent packing by these two weird kids too.

28

"Okay," Harry replied.

He turned and walked away. He looked over his shoulder only once and saw the boy and the little girl hug one another. Something about the way they acted towards one another made Harry think they were brother and sister.

"Something's just not right with them," Harry said.

Beside him, only seen by Harry, Rabbit

nodded his head. "Indeed," Rabbit said. "I'd go so far as to say that there could be something very wrong."

"You think they need help?" Harry asked.

"From time to time, everyone needs a little help." Rabbit said. "It's just a matter of figuring out how to give that help."

Harry thought about this as he passed through the gate, got on his bike, and started pedaling back toward town. This time when he passed Folly Farm, he made sure to stay on the other side of the road. But even though he was very aware of being on Mayor Kilgore's property, his mind was back at the carnival with the two kids behind the lion cage.

29

Once again, Clive Cantaloni's Carnival and Magic Show was the topic of conversation around the Moon dinner table. Only this time, there was a little less excitement and a lot more concern. Harry told his parents and

Honey about how Mr. Cantaloni had shut him down and then about the two kids he'd seen.

"That is a very bothersome story, Harry. Are you sure the children seemed like they were out of place?" Mary asked.

"I thought they did for sure," Harry said. "The thing I don't understand is that I *know* the little girl was crying. Even if they *didn't* work there, why would they lie about being okay?"

30

"Well, we can't just assume things," John Moon said. "You know, your grandma used to have a saying about assuming things. I can't quite remember it at the moment, though."

"Yes," Mary Moon added. "I'd certainly hate to report this to the police and it ends up being nothing. That could cause Mr. Cantaloni unnecessary trouble. Is there anything else you can think of that you saw that might clue you into the fact that these kids were in some sort of trouble?"

Harry thought long and hard about it but

could come up with nothing. Maybe if he hadn't been so devastated by the rejection from the mighty Mr. Cantaloni, he would have been able to judge the situation better.

"You know, Harry," John Moon said. "It could be it's just part of the act. Maybe those kids are involved in some really cool part of the carnival that we can't even imagine."

"I don't know, Dad," Harry replied, doubtfully. "You didn't see them. Something wasn't right."

Sitting across from Harry, Honey had remained quiet for the entire conversation and decided to finally speak up. When she did, Harry was surprised at the anger in her voice.

"It wouldn't surprise me if those kids *are* in some sort of trouble," she blared. "If a man has no problem caging up those beautiful, big cats, maybe he doesn't have a problem with keeping kids in cages!"

"Now, Honey . . ." Mary started.

31

"I'm sorry, Mom . . . but I have to do *something*. And I think I know what, now! I was reading in the library today and came across the idea of maybe trying to start a petition."

"A petition for what?" Harry asked.

"To shut down that stinky, old carnival!"

Harry didn't like this idea. Sure, he was still upset about the abrupt way Mr. Cantaloni had spoken to him, but he wasn't ready to protest the carnival because of it. "Classic Honey Moon overreach," he said. "We aren't even sure what's going on over there."

"Is it?" she asked. "Well, I *do* know for sure those poor animals don't deserve such treatment, and I'm going to see to it that they are freed! I might even call up the news station!"

With Honey's rant over, Mary Moon looked thoughtfully at her son.

"We can't let those two kids go unnoticed,

Harry," she said. "So maybe we'll keep an eye out for them on Saturday. Okay?"

"Yeah, sounds good," Harry replied.

But the thought of the kids would not leave his head. And he didn't know if he would be able to wait until Saturday to get to the bottom of things. Even though they shook their heads *no*, he felt that somehow those scrawny, scared kids needed him. And to borrow an expression from his own sister, Harry needed to go where he was needed.

33

When dinner was over, he'd call his pals Bailey, Declan, and Hao. If anyone could get some answers, it was the Good Mischief Team!

34

UNDER THE COVER OF NIGHT

The boys met at the Pumpkin Patch just after eleven o'clock. It was Friday night, so they were not worried about showing up to school tired the next day. Still, they met knowing that all of their parents would give them a good grounding if they knew their kids were sneaking out at night. All around them, their sleepy, little town was quiet and peaceful.

To jump-start their adventure, they huddled together in the middle of the patch and whispered the *Good Mischief Anthem*. It was their way of getting pumped for whatever might occur. The air was thin. That meant voices carried. They spoke in a low hush.

We don't fight with sticks and stones
We don't want to break your bones
We have a much more ingenious scheme
We are the Good Mischief Team!

Might does not make right,
So when we take on the epic fight
We are trained to follow the gleam
We are the Good Mischief Team!

We never like to make things tragic
We use reason, heart, and magic
We take the lead from the brightest dream
For we are the Good Mischief Team!
Rah, rah, hurrah!

Their huddle finished, they stood beside their bikes and looked toward the black forms of the carnival tents standing against the moonlit,

36

gray horizon. Even though the anthem always helped buoy the boys' spirits up, apprehension remained in the air.

"Are you sure about this, Harry?" Declan asked.

"No," Harry replied. "If the gate is locked, we'll have to climb over it. And that's . . ."

"That's trespassing," Hao said.

"Against the law," Bailey added.

"Well, let's go check that gate," Bailey asked. He was usually the most adventurous of the team. He always preferred to act first and ask questions later.

The four boys pedaled quickly through the night. When they passed Folly Farm, Harry glanced over to Mayor Kligore's house on the hill. A single light was on upstairs, making Harry wonder what sort of devious activities the mayor might be up to at such a late hour.

Before they knew it, the dark shape of the carnival gate was upon them. They slowed to a stop. Baily jumped from his bike. He ran to the gate. He discovered the gate was unlocked. As if to make sure he wasn't seeing things, Bailey gave it a little push, and it swung open a little more.

"Okay, let's go, men," Bailey said.

"So are we really going to do this?" Declan asked.

No one replied. But Harry saw the two kids in his mind. He saw how scared and dirty they had been. And every time he remembered it, the more certain he was that something bad was going on there and he was needed.

"Yes, we're doing this," Harry said. He took the lead.

Overhead, the moon was full, throwing an eerie glow across the fairgrounds. From what Harry could tell, the place was all set up and ready to go for tomorrow. A Ferris wheel had been erected, as had a few more games and food booths.

"Wow. This place is sort of creepy at night, huh?" Declan asked.

The three others nodded in agreement as they pushed their bikes through the grounds. The place was so quiet that Harry could hear the loud purring of sleeping tigers and lions from somewhere in the darkness. He heard a soft, whistling noise from somewhere else. Although he had no idea what a sleeping elephant sounded like, Harry Moon thought that was what he was hearing.

To his right, Harry saw the truck that the kids had been hiding behind earlier. The truck had moved, and he wasn't at all surprised when he did not find the kids behind it.

40

"I don't get it," Declan said. "If there *are* kids being held as workers by this Cantaloni guy, wouldn't they have gone home like all of the other workers?"

"Maybe," Harry said. "Unless they don't have a home."

"Or maybe he makes them sleep in a stable or cages like the animals," Hao suggested.

Harry didn't like to think of those two kids sleeping in such conditions, but once Hao had planted the idea, it would not leave his head.

"Oh no, Harry," Hao said, apparently seeing the thoughtful look on his face. "I was just kidding."

"I know," Harry said. "But maybe that's where we should check."

"Well, where do the animals sleep?" Bailey asked.

Harry shrugged but cocked his ear to the right. He was pretty sure the sounds of the sleeping cats were coming from that direction. They wound around a row of games—a miniature bowling alley, a knock-the-bottles-over game, and something with water guns—toward the back of the site. Harry saw all kinds of cords and wires running to a pair of generators hiding behind a huge painting of clowns and smiling kids. The generators were all off, like weird sleeping robots in the dark.

Sure enough, after questing another few moments, they came to what looked like a large but poorly constructed barn. There were several cages outside of it, but they were all empty. In front of the barn, there was a large pen filled with hay.

"Yuck," Bailey said. "You guys smell that?"

"Yeah," Declan said, covering his nose. "That's pretty ripe."

Harry smelled it too. It was from where all of the animals were forced to use the bathroom in the same place. He wrinkled his nose at the smell and, not for the first time, wondered if maybe Honey was on to something. Maybe keeping all of these animals in cages and puny little barn-like structures was worse than he thought.

The four boys looked around the barn but could not find a way in. A series of small windows ran along the top, but it would be impossible (and dangerous) to get in.

"Well, now what?" Declan asked.

"Maybe we just go home," Harry said. "The gate was open, which means there's someone here. And I'd rather not get caught."

"Same here," Bailey said. They stood near the pen in front of the barn, looking out at the fairgrounds. Despite his disappointment and fear in that moment, Harry couldn't deny how excited he was to come here tomorrow when everything was in full swing.

"So, are you guys ready?" Hao asked.

"Yeah," Declan said. "We better—"

43

A growling sound from behind made them all freeze. They turned around in unison at the menacing noise. They stared directly into the eyes of an enormous lion. Only the flimsy boards of the fence separated them, and when the lion bared its teeth and roared at them, those boards seemed weak indeed.

The roar seemed to shake their bikes. The bared teeth of the lion caused the team to scream in terror. Harry didn't think he had ever moved so fast as he hopped on his bike and pedaled furiously toward the gate.

Behind them, the lion let out another roar. Harry tore through the night on his bike, leading his three best friends directly out of harm's way.

As they made their way back to the front of the fairgrounds where the steel Octopus looked like monstrous tentacles in the night, they heard another noise from behind them. This time, it was a man's voice.

"Hey! What are you kids doing there?"

The voice was gruff, loud, and insistent. Instantly, Harry knew the source. But, Harry was working on pure fear and didn't even consider stopping to answer the question. His legs continued to pump, the bike's pedals now just a blur in the darkness. He sped toward the gate and slipped right between it and the post. When he was out on Witch Boom Road with his friends behind him, he could feel the piercing eyes of Clive Cantaloni staring at him from the cartoon sign above the iron gate.

Harry's heart hammered in his chest. The

boys sped on, not slowing up until the Pumpkin Patch was in sight. When they finally came to a stop, the Good Mischief Team was all wild-eyed. They hunkered down behind the pumpkins. The town was still quiet, but after what they had just been through, they weren't about to take the chance of being spotted by anyone.

"That was pretty intense!" Bailey said in an excited whisper.

45

"Scary is what it was," Hao added.

"Sorry, guys," Harry said. "I shouldn't have asked you to come. We probably shouldn't have done that at all."

"Are you kidding?" Declan said. "I just stared a lion right in the face and lived through it. If you ask me, that's as epic as it gets!"

"Whatever it was," Harry said, "we should get back home before our folks find out we're gone."

"Good idea," Declan said.

"See you guys tomorrow," Harry said in a hush.

"Yeah . . . at the carnival right?" Hao asked.

The four boys laughed nervously at this as they pedaled out of the Pumpkin Patch and headed for their Sleepy Hollow homes.

46

∾

Harry lay in his bed half an hour later, staring up at the ceiling. He felt guilty for sneaking out on his parents, but he felt that it had been necessary. He really did feel strongly about those two kids—and the more he thought about them, the more certain he was that they needed his help, even if they had pushed him away earlier in the day.

As he drifted off to sleep, Harry Moon envisioned the great robe of some formidable ghost hovering before him. Beneath the robes of the ghost stood two children, a boy and a girl. Harry shook his head, trying to rattle the vision from his head.

"Rabbit?" Harry called out from his dark bedroom.

"Yes, Harry?"

Rabbit hopped out of the shadows and took a seat at the edge of the bed. He nestled down and got comfortable, snuggling up next to Harry's feet.

"Sneaking out on Mom and Dad tonight . . . that was bad, huh?"

"It wasn't the best choice you've ever made," Rabbit said. "On the other hand, your intentions were good."

"I just can't stop thinking about what sort of trouble those kids might be in. Now, I am having dreams about them."

"I know," Rabbit said.

"What do you think is wrong with them?" Harry asked.

Rabbit thought for a while before answering. "They seemed lost, didn't they?"

Lost, Harry thought. He wouldn't have thought to use that word. He'd thought they simply looked scared. But now that he could again see their faces in his mind, he thought lost fit quite well.

48

As he thought about this, another idea came to him. This one was even worse than thinking the kids were being held at the carnival against their will.

What if they *were* lost? What if there weren't supposed to be on those fairgrounds at all?

THE SLEEPY HOLLOW MAGIC SHOPPE

H arry wasted no time the following day. Because he was usually out of the door as soon as possible on Saturdays, he was pretty sure his parents thought nothing of him leaving the moment he wolfed down his pancakes. They also knew that he was still very excited about attending the carnival later in the day.

So with a quick series of goodbyes and a messy kiss from Harvest, Harry was out the door and into the Saturday morning sunshine before most young boys his age were rolling out of bed. He made a direct line toward the Sleepy Hollow Magic Shoppe, eager to tell his friend and mentor, Samson Dupree, about the two kids at the fairgrounds.

Harry arrived at the shop just as Samson was unlocking the door and flipping the sign in his window from CLOSED to OPEN. Samson cracked open the door for Harry and ushered him inside. As usual, Samson was wearing a purple robe and his red slippers. His face held the same friendly yet wise countenance Harry had grown to love. Of course, Harry never tired of the shop, either. He could stay inside all day, just staring at the potions, books, and magical objects. The Sleepy Hollow Magic Shoppe was like a second home for Harry Moon.

"Good morning, Harry! What brings you out so early?" Samson asked. "Something tells me that it may have to do with our visitors, Clive Cantaloni's Carnival and Magic Show."

"It does," Harry said. "But maybe not in the way you're thinking."

"Really?" Samson asked as he walked behind his counter and powered up his

register for the day. "I thought if anyone in Sleepy Hollow would be looking forward to the carnival, it would be you. Clive Cantaloni is a great showman. He's no Elvis Gold, but he's quite good."

"Oh, I'm still looking forward to it," Harry said. "Very much, in fact. But I was over at the fairgrounds yesterday and saw something that upset me."

"Is that so?" Samson asked, leaning over the counter and looking into Harry's face. He knew his friend was very sensitive to matters of light and dark and so always paid special attention to Harry's concerns.

Yes," Harry replied. He figured he'd skip over the part where Mr. Cantaloni had flat-out rejected him for the magic show. Anyway, Samson probably knew that already. Harry had come to understand that his eccentrically dressed friend had powers Harry could only dream about.

Instead, Harry reported about the incident that continued to amp his imagination. "There were these two kids out there on Friday afternoon, hiding behind one of the lion cages. They looked sort of sad, dirty, and just flat out of place."

"Do you feel that they weren't just part of the act?"

"I guess they could be," Harry admitted. "But I really don't think so. There were a young girl and a boy a little older than her. I think they were brother and sister. I asked them if they were okay, but they sort of just asked me to scram. But the weirdest thing is that I dreamt about them."

53

"Oh, what kind of dream was it? Tell me."

"Well, there was a large ghost in a green robe, and he lifted the folds of his garment, and there were the two children. One boy. One girl. They looked very much like the kids at the carnival." As Harry spoke, the light of recognition appeared in Samson's eyes. He smiled with kindness at the boy.

"Come with me, Harry," said Samson. The proprietor walked through the velvet-curtained door behind the register. Harry followed him to his study. This is where Samson Dupree kept his library of books, his special laboratory of herbs and oils, and an old globe of the world made of fine stone.

He stepped onto a ladder to reach a thin, leather-bound book on one of the top shelves. The binding had its share of dust, and so Samson shook it clean. With great respect, he placed the little book on his polished, oak desk and opened it so that Harry and he could review it together.

"You know this book well," said Samson, smiling, as he fingered the edges of the title page to reveal that it was a first edition of Charles Dickens's *A Christmas Carol*. Its date of publication was 1843.

"Yes," Harry said with a grin. He was a little surprised that the book was not a book on spells or potions. "I have read it several times. It doesn't matter what grade I'm in, the English

teachers all love it."

"As they should," said Samson as he turned the pages. "It is a tale for all ages about the power of the Christmas Spirit. Ever since Charlie penned the tale and the people of the world read it, Christmas has become a time of charitable giving. This is in part because of what the Ghost of Christmas Present held beneath his robe."

"What he had under his robe?" Harry asked. He tried to remember the Christmas Present portion of the story.

"There were two children beneath the great robe. Scrooge saw them. The image of them startled Ebenezer," said Samson as he looked down at the book. The old proprietor put his index finger to one particular page searching for the passage. "Oh, yes. Here it is. 'From the foldings of its robe, it brought two children; wretched, abject, frightful, hideous, miserable. They knelt down at its feet, and clung upon the outside of its garment. "Oh, Man! look here. Look, look, down here!" exclaimed

55

the Ghost. They were a boy and girl. Yellow, meagre, ragged, scowling, wolfish.'"

"Who were these children, Samson?" Harry asked. Samson looked up. "I mean, who were they in the story Dickens told?"

"Dickens said they were the children of the world. They were named *Want* and *Ignorance*. Dickens's thinking was that these children were the responsibility of everyone. That no one is alone. That the poor, the minimalized, the cripples, and the orphans are all our shared responsibility. We live with them. They are part of our lives.

"Because of this visit by the Ghost of Christmas Present, Ebenezer Scrooge saw his own responsibility to take care of his employee's crippled son, Tiny Tim. That night changed Scrooge. The visit by the two children changed him," said Samson.

Harry thought about this for a moment. He did his best thinking while in Samson's magic shop.

"So why, Harry, do the two children that you saw briefly at the carnival haunt you?"

Harry shook his head; he didn't really know the reason why.

"Maybe, because like Ebenezer Scrooge, you are being awakened to your own responsibility to help them."

Harry nodded. "It was just as Rabbit told me."

57

"And what was it that Rabbit told you?" Samson asked with a smile.

"That from time to time, everyone needs a little help," Harry replied.

"Precisely! Things happen for a reason, Harry. I believe you discovered those two children because you have a part to play in their lives. Now, as Rabbit says, you will need to figure that out for yourself."

Harry nodded. Samson always had a way

of making Harry feel more at ease without delivering cheesy pep talks. "Will I see you at the carnival?" Harry asked.

"You might, indeed. I never knew a funnel cake that disagreed with me." Samson smiled.

"Thanks, Samson."

"Of course, Harry."

Deep in his thoughts, Harry made his way back out of the study and the magic shop. He was so distracted by his thoughts that he barely saw the news van rolling up Main Street. The words, *Action News*, were painted on the side.

Oh no, he thought. *Did Honey actually call the news?*

He got his answer when he noticed Honey blazing up the street on her bike and behind the van. The wind was blowing her hair back. She looked like a girl on a mission.

"Oh, that's just great," Harry said, dashing in her direction.

Harry had chosen not to take his bike out that morning, still spinning from the encounter with the lion the night before. Without his bike, he had to run very fast across Main Street and through the town square under the dark shadow of the Headless Horseman. He just barely made it, catching up with Honey as she reeled to a stop, apparently winded from trying to keep up with the much faster news van.

As she caught her breath while leaning over the handlebars, she and Harry watched the news van carry on toward Melville Field where the tops of the tents still stood tall.

"What are you doing?" Harry asked.

"I told you last night, Harold," she said, gasping for breath. "I'm going to see that those wonderful, big cats are set free! I started a petition online last night and called the news people."

"Honey . . . you're going to cause so much trouble!"

"You said yourself that you think there's something fishy going on with that stupid carnival. I'm going to do something about it!"

"Yeah, but—"

60

"It's too late, anyway, brothere," Honey said. "I already have over one hundred signatures on the Honey Moon petition, and the news is all over it already! The Action News team is going to grill that mean, old Clive Cantaloni!"

Harry was going to continue his argument but never got a chance. Honey saw one of her friends from school across the street and waved her down.

"Claire! Claire! Come over here and sign my petition."

Without giving Harry another second of her

time, not even with a "goodbye" or a "see ya later," Honey zoomed across the street toward Claire and several other girls. Harry watched her go, shaking his head.

He turned his attention back to the shapes of the tents poking up over the horizon in Melville Field. He knew he had another three hours before the gates would open and the carnival would begin . . . if the news crews and Honey's dumb petition didn't get in the way.

He decided to walk over to Declan's house to waste those three hours away. As he hung out with his buddy playing video games, Harry continued to get more and more excited about the carnival. Today had the potential to be one of those awesome days that he and his friends would talk about forever. But he also still felt the creeping sensation that something shady was happening at the fairgrounds and that he was supposed to do *something* to help those two kids. And uncomfortably, that feeling of responsibility felt much bigger than his opportunity to have fun.

62

WELCOME TO
THE CIRCUS

When Harry, Declan, Bailey, and Hao arrived at the entrance to the carnival, the dusty parking lot was already jammed with cars. They'd arrived fifteen minutes early, hoping to beat the crowds. They made their way beyond the parking lot and headed to the ticket booth. They each paid their ten bucks to get in. As they traveled beneath the great iron gate and stepped into the carnival grounds, a sense of wonder washed over Harry.

"Whoa," Declan said. "This is *awesome*."

He was right. As Harry looked around, there were hundreds of things he wanted to check out. There were dozens of games to play, all being announced by energetic barkers yelling out news about instructions and prizes. The smells of various sticky foods were wafting out of a seemingly endless string of food vendors. A few clowns were darting through the gathering crowd. They handed out balloons to the younger kids.

The calliope music Harry heard yesterday was louder now. Like a breeze, it passed through the fairgrounds. He saw smiles every-where, on kids and parents alike. Everyone was cheering and laughing, making it very hard for Harry to believe that there might be something nefarious lurking underneath it all.

When the Good Mischief Team saw the big

steel octopus, they took their place in line. The ride looked awesome. Its mechanical tentacles lifted little booths into the air. Kids screamed with delight as the arms went up and down, up and down. Harry and his pals were no different when it was their turn. As Harry found himself whirled up into the air, he tried to remember to keep an eye out for the two kids he'd spotted behind the lion cage yesterday. But as the carnival swept him away with its fun and games, the two kids were very far from his mind.

65

After the Octopus, they each got a candied apple and then walked over to where several clowns were making balloon animals. From there they played several games. As it turned out, Declan was pretty good at the ring toss and ended up winning a cool slingshot for a prize. There was so much to see and do that Harry wondered how anyone could experience it all in a single day.

As they walked deeper into the carnival, Harry spotted the truck where he'd seen the two kids cowering. His heart sank. He felt guilty for almost forgetting about them. By the trucks, he saw people from the Action News. A cameraman filmed a reporter that seemed to be checking out one of the empty cages that were attached behind the truck.

"What is it, Harry?" Declan asked.

Harry blinked, realizing that he had been staring at the news crew and the empty cages. He started to scan the crowd for any signs of the two kids but saw none. There were so many children running around that picking just two out of the group would be next to impossible.

"Nothing," Harry replied.

Just then, a booming voice filled the air, replacing the calliope music that had been playing. It was obvious the voice rumbled from the speakers attached to the tall poles scattered throughout the carnival. Everyone looked up at those big speakers as Mr. Cantaloni himself addressed his crowd.

"Come one, come all! Witness the one and

only Clive Cantaloni Magic Show and Carnival Fun extravaganza! It'll be taking place in the red big top tent in exactly fifteen minutes! Get there early and grab a good seat because you are *not* going to want to miss this!"

With the announcement over, the calliope music returned, and the crowd started moving around again. Most of them were headed directly for the red tent Harry had visited yesterday.

"That sounds right up your alley, Harry," Hao said. "Let's go. It sounds awesome."

"Oh yeah!" Bailey said.

The four boys headed that way, and although Harry was excited about the show, he now made an extra effort to check around for the boy and girl he had seen yesterday. He also recalled Mr. Cantaloni's words in the back of his head, remembering how mean he had been yesterday. *Was he really mean, or are you just upset that he's not giving you a shot?* Harry asked himself. He honestly wasn't

67

sure.

They made their way into the tent and managed to get decent seats. They saw lots of familiar faces from school. Harry even spotted his parents filing into the tent. His father was holding Harvest, who had his face buried in a sticky cloud of pink cotton candy. They all waved at Harry. Harvest used his cotton-covered fingers to do so.

68

As they waited for the show to begin, Harry spotted Honey. She walked up and down the aisles on the other side of the tent, waving her petition in the faces of anyone that would listen to her. Harry quickly looked away, hoping she wouldn't spot him or the Good Mischief Team.

Finally, drums beat from somewhere within the tent. Lights flickered across the large, open ring at the center of the huge tent. The audience cheered in anticipation. After several moments, there was a loud crash of cymbals.

Clive Cantaloni walked out to the center of the ring. He held a microphone in his hand.

Under the spotlight, he looked like a snow-capped mountain with his tall, wide figure and dense, white tresses. Then Harry saw something he had not been expecting. There was a parrot sitting on Clive's shoulder. The bird was bright with color—lime green, butter yellow, and fire-engine red.

"Good evening ladies and gentlemen, boys and girls," he said. "And welcome to Clive Cantaloni's Carnival and Magic Show!"

He then placed the microphone in front of the parrot. It pecked at it for a moment and then said: "Welcome." *Squawk!* "Enjoy the carnival." *Squawk!*

The crowd applauded. Kids cheered and laughed. The parrot squawked a few more times and then launched itself from Mr. Cantaloni's shoulders. He took several laps around the tent. The parrot nearly touched the heads of those in the top row. When the parrot was finished with his flight, he settled back on Mr. Cantaloni's shoulder.

"Now, I'd like to introduce you to some more of my favorite friends," Mr. Cantaloni said.

With that, he clapped his hands a few times and pointed to the far side of the tent. As Harry watched, he noticed that the cameramen and anchorwoman from Action News were stationed at the rim of the ring. He wondered what sort of spin the news team would give the story. Would they cover the fact that everyone seemed to be having fun or that there were caged animals being used as entertainment?

Harry turned his attention to the floor where a small parade of animals arrived through a set of curtains at the far side of the tent. For the next twenty minutes, this amazing animal parade carried the show. Three monkeys did cartwheels and juggled a series of balls and bananas. They were followed by a tiny dog pushing a skateboard. He did a few tricks on a ramp, complete with a flip. Two tigers appeared, each jumping through a hoop. They then settled down on the floor by Mr. Cantaloni as if they were simple household cats.

Next came the lion. When Harry and his pals saw it, they went tense. They shared an uneasy look. Declan appeared absolutely terrified. The lion took the center of the ring. He let out a mighty roar. Mr. Cantaloni approached, holding his hand out. He then pulled a ball out of his pocket and held his hands behind his back. He made a big show of shuffling the ball around from hand to hand behind his back. When he extended his closed hands to him, the lion sniffed them for a moment and then gently placed its large paw on one of Mr. Cantaloni's hands. There was the ball.

The lion did this three times and got it correct each time. The king of the jungle followed this up by performing a series of tricks where he stood on its back legs and walked several feet like a human. He also ate a small strip of jerky from Mr. Cantaloni's mouth before letting the two monkeys ride him around the floor like a horse.

The crowd was thrilled. They ate up every moment of it. Harry spotted Honey over by

71

their parents and saw that she was not pleased at all. She was wearing what Mary Moon called her *pouting face*. Harry wondered if Honey had overstepped her bounds with her enthusiasm. While the lion and tigers were being used for entertainment, they seemed well cared for and respected. What was Honey thinking? *She was going to get the cats released . . . and then what? Live on Nightingale Lane with them, letting the big cats share the dinner bowl with the family dog, Half Moon?* Harry sighed, remembering Honey was just a kid.

Clive Cantaloni stepped back to the center of the floor, taking a bow. "Now," he said, his voice booming through the speaker system, "it is time to bring out one of my very special friends. Ladies and gentlemen, boys and girls, I'd like for you to meet Flo."

All eyes returned to the large curtains. Something slowly rippled the curtains. A huge elephant marched into the ring. When the elephant's head was free of the curtains, she stretched out her ears, raised her trunk, and blared a loud trumpeting sound. On her back

was a red-and-white, striped saddle.

When she reached the center of the ring, the elephant went to her stomach in a clumsy sort of way. She turned to face Mr. Cantaloni. The ring leader stroked the elephant's head, whispered something into her ear, and then climbed up the steps on the saddle. Within seconds, he was mounted on the elephant's back.

"Good girl, Flo!" Cantaloni cheered.

With that, Flo got to her feet and continued marching around the ring of the big top floor. After she had made a lap, Mr. Cantaloni stroked her on the head. Into his microphone, he asked her, "How about a nap now, Flo?"

74

Flo shook her large head. Her ears flapped comically back and forth.

"Are you sure?" Mr. Cantaloni asked.

This time, Flo nodded. The crowd roared with laughter as Mr. Cantaloni looked at them and shrugged.

"Now, Flo . . . you know that performing for all of these people can take it out of you. You really should rest. Maybe it's the lights. Is it too bright in here for you?"

She nodded again and gave another great

trumpeting from her trunk.

"Fine then," he said. "Someone in the control booth, can we do something about these lights?"

For five seconds or so, nothing happened. But then in the blink of an eye, all of the lights within the tent went out. The crowd *oohed* and *ahhed*. Even Harry found himself in suspense about what might happen next.

The lights remained out, and from the floor, Mr. Cantaloni could be heard whispering into the microphone. "Flo? What on earth? Flo? FLO? Someone, please, cut the lights back on!"

The light snapped back on. Hundreds of surprised gasps filled the stands as the floor lit up.

Flo was nowhere to be seen.

Harry could tell from the look on Mr. Cantaloni's face that this was all part of the

75

act. There was a smile lurking under his fake fear. He made a show of looking around like she might be hiding somewhere within plain sight and then shrugged.

"You know," he said to the crowd, "she does this from time to time. Stage fright, I think."

A few nervous chuckles passed through the crowd as Mr. Cantaloni still pretended to look for Flo. "Okay . . . I think I know what do to. Someone in the control booth, can you cut the lights out again?"

Once again, the lights went out. This time, they remained out for a good twenty seconds. A small flame ran around the ring of the floor, enveloping the stage in a perfect circle of fire.

Sure enough, the flames illuminated Flo at the center. Not only that, but Mr. Cantaloni was again seated on her back. A small spotlight shined down from overhead. It was the only additional light source other than the circle of flames.

"Thank you, Flo!"

The mighty elephant rose onto on her back legs, Mr. Cantaloni strapped onto the saddle. As she trumpeted, the crowd applauded.

"And now for Flo's next trick . . ."

But that's as far as Clive Cantaloni got. Someone down in the front of the ring screamed. Soon after, others were yelling and shouting. Even from farther up where Harry was sitting, there was a single word that was easy to pick out from the mad scramble below.

"Fire!"

Harry looked around and saw that there was indeed a fire at one of the curtained entrances to the tent. Dozens of people dashed from their seats toward the exits that were free of flames. As more and more people realized what was happening, the fire grew larger. Flames licked along the lower bleachers.

"Everyone, please file out as orderly as possible," Mr. Cantaloni shouted from the microphone. Flo bellowed in agreement.

All of a sudden, several security officers from the carnival rushed down the aisles, making certain everyone made it out safely. Harry, Declan, Bailey, and Hao headed into their aisle and followed a security guard down the stands and out of the tent.

But even before they were outside, the tent had started to fill with smoke. Harry knew that the rest of his family was in there and started to fear the worst.

Up In Smoke

Harry was amazed at how fast things progressed. Within minutes, he saw Honey emerge from the tent. A few seconds behind her, Harry's mom and dad exited. His dad carried Harvest. Harvest was coughing softly and pointing back towards the tent with little tears trailing down his face.

Harry dashed over to them and received

huge embraces from his parents.

"Are you okay?" Mary Moon asked.

"Yes, I'm fine," Harry said. "Do you think everyone got out in time?"

"I think so. Most people were out before us," John said.

Behind them, a Sleepy Hollow fire truck pulled up next to the tent. Several firemen, led by Chief Mike Orize, jumped down from the truck. Some dashed inside the tent, carrying the long hose that was still attached to the fire truck. Security guards made sure everyone backed away from the tent while the fire department did their work.

Harry could hear all sorts of commotion from the other side of the tent. He heard tigers and lions roaring and the urgent bellows of Flo.

"Oh no!" Honey screamed. "The animals!"

She took off so fast that neither of her

parents was able to stop her. Harry went behind her, worried that she'd not pay attention because she was so worried about the animals.

As he followed her to the back of the tent, there was commotion everywhere. Firefighters and security guards scrambled. Carnival-goers dashed to get out of the way. Smoke billowed up into the air, and the smell of burning things started to get thick.

When Honey made it to the back of the tent, Harry finally managed to catch up with her. They got there just in time to see Mr. Cantaloni helping a very panicked tiger into a cage a safe distance away from the tent. Behind him, three trainers worked with Flo to make sure she remained as calm as possible.

Harry also saw that the Action News team was capturing it all on film. Behind them, the firefighters continued to battle the blaze inside the tent. He could hear the water splashing and the voices of the firefighters from inside. From what Harry could tell, they had managed to get the better of the fire before it had a chance to do any real damage.

"You old meanie!" Honey shouted, shaking a finger at Mr. Cantaloni. "How can you keep these beautiful animals in cages? How can you endanger their lives like this?"

"Little girl, I have their best interests at heart," he said. "I love all of them as if they were my own children. Might I suggest you get back to your parents while our brave firefighters get the fire under control?"

"He's right," Harry said. "Come on, Honey. Let's get back to Mom and Dad."

"But the animals!"

"They're okay," Harry said. "And your news people are catching it all anyway."

It broke his heart a little to see that Honey was crying as he led her away from the back of the tent. As they returned to their parents, Harry saw that things were dying down a little. He watched as the firemen bravely did their duty, rushing in and out of the still-smoking tent. On one side of the tent, Harry saw one of the emergency workers placing an oxygen mask over a girl Harry knew from school. Fortunately, it seemed to be the worst that had happened.

He watched the EMT workers and the firefighters with awe. He had stepped into Clive Cantaloni's tent for a magic show and had ended up witnessing acts of bravery from people that lived and worked right within Sleepy Hollow.

As he watched all of this, taking great pride in the tight-knit sense of community in his town, Harry caught a brief glimpse of two familiar faces in the crowd.

It was the two kids from yesterday.

They were standing behind the merry-go-round, watching as the commotion settled. They watched with fear in their eyes.

Slowly, Harry started to walk toward them. He hoped he might be able to sneak up beside them before they were aware that he had spotted them. He made his way through the thinning crowd, stepping through thin trails of smoke that still escaped the seams of the big, red tent.

Just as he neared the front end of the merry-go-round, the boy spotted him. For a moment, Harry and the boy locked eyes through the legs of a large, white, wooden horse. But the merry-go-round continued to turn. When another wooden horse moved past him, Harry discovered the boy and girl were gone.

"Wait!" Harry yelled.

He darted around the side of the merry-go-round to chase after them. But by the time he reached the other side, he could no longer see them. They had disappeared into the crowd.

Disappointed, Harry turned around and nearly bumped into the man that was standing behind him.

"Excuse me," Harry said apologetically.

When he peered up at the tall figure, his heart froze. Looking down into his face was none other than Mayor Maximus Kligore! The mayor sneered at Harry as if he'd just been bitten by some pesky insect.

"Well, Mr. Harry Moon," the mayor snarled. "I should have known you would have been here. You and your silly magic would fit in nicely here, wouldn't it?"

Any other time, Harry would have been intimidated and maybe even a little angry about the mayor speaking to him in such a way. But right now, all Harry could think about were those two kids.

"I don't suppose *you* had anything to do with this fire, did you?" Mayor Kligore asked.

"What?" Harry asked, shocked. "Are you serious?"

"Well, of course, I am. After all, you're the best known magician in Sleepy Hollow. Maybe the thought of a much better show coming onto your turf made you upset."

"That's ridiculous," Harry said. "I thought the show was great until . . . well, until the fire."

"It was alright," he said. "A great revenue boost to Sleepy Hollow. But I hear that you were out here yesterday before the show was even open."

Harry said nothing. He wondered how the mayor had heard about his failed meeting with Clive Cantaloni. He guessed the mayor had eyes everywhere.

"Fortunately for you, Harry Moon, I have far too much on my plate right now. I must pretend to care about the well-being of all of these people. Run along, Moon-boy. I'm sure you and I will have much to discuss the *next* time we meet."

87

There always seems to be a next time with this guy, Harry thought. He gave the mayor a distrustful look and then turned away.

He looked and looked, but he could not see the two kids. After looking around the game booths, the food stands, and the still-scrambling people that had escaped the tent, he found his friends. They were huddled around a booth that sold funnel cakes. He even saw Samson there, taking a huge bite out of a cake covered in heaps of powdered sugar. Samson gave Harry a wink, shook his head, and stepped back out into the crowd.

"You okay?" Declan asked him.

"Yeah, I'm fine," Harry said.

"You sure?" Hao asked.

From behind him, he heard another familiar voice. "Well, you don't look fine, kiddo."

It was John Moon. Mary, Honey, and Harvest were all with him. They looked tired and a little sad about how the day's events had turned out.

"What do you say we all head home?" John asked. "I think there's been enough excitement at the carnival today."

"Yeah, I guess so," Harry said.

They grabbed some candied apples from a booth. As the family walked back toward the gate, Harry still found himself looking around the crowd for the two kids. But there was no sign of them. It was almost like they were ghosts.

A New Recruit

On Sunday, as the Moon Family made their way into church, Harry heard whispers. Everyone was talking about the fiasco at the carnival yesterday. Through the whispers, Harry gathered a few things about the outcome of Saturday's events.

Most importantly, no one had been hurt. The heroic firefighters, under Chief Orize's direction, had managed to extinguish the flames before anyone had been wounded. Also, very little damage had been done to Clive Cantaloni's property. He might spend most of his Sunday patching up the top of his big, red tent but other than that, he had been fortunate.

Harry ran the events of yesterday afternoon through his head as Pastor Josh went through a sermon on the Tower of Babel. The fire and smoke had been a little scary, for sure, but Harry was still very worried about the two kids. He simply couldn't get their faces out of his mind. He decided then and there, just as Pastor Josh was about to go into the closing prayer, that he had to do something. *But what?* he thought.

When the Moons returned home, they discovered something quite interesting on their porch. It was a flier featuring Clive Cantaloni's smiling face. He was smoking a cigar and, just like Harry had seen up-close and personal, the puffs of smoke created a parrot-cloud above his head.

Under the caricature of Clive Cantaloni's face, there was a letter. It read:

Lovely Sleepy Hollow Residents,

Did you happen to attend my Carnival and Magic Show yesterday? If you did, then you probably know about the unfortunate mishap that occurred during the big top show. While such a terrible mistake has never been made during one of my shows, these sorts of things DO happen to even the greatest of showmen from time to time. I was extremely fortunate that no one was hurt, including Flo and the rest of my amazing animals!

As you may or may not know, the carnival is in town all week. And because yesterday was such a mess, I am offering FREE ADMISSION to anyone that brings their ticket stub from Saturday. Please consider this an apology for yesterday's mistakes and a gesture of appreciation for your business.

Kind regards,
Clive Cantaloni

91

"Well, that's nice of him," John Moon said.

"Can we go back today?" Harry asked.

"I don't know," Mary said. "Yesterday was so . . . well, so *awful*. Why don't we take a break from the carnival and see what the week brings? Maybe we could all go one day after school."

"Hmmph," Honey said. "I don't want to go back. Did you *see* those poor animals?"

"They looked pretty happy to me," Harry said.

"Don't start, you two," Mary said.

Honey was still grumbling as they walked inside. Harry was holding the flier and remembering the brief conversation he'd had with Mr. Cantaloni on Friday. *Maybe he isn't such a bad guy, after all,* he thought. *This invitation is a really nice gesture.*

Even with the excitement of a possible visit

to the carnival again later in the week, Harry was still bothered by the thought of the two kids he had not yet been able to really speak to. He knew they needed help and that he was the one to help them. How had Dickens described the children of Christmas present? *They were a boy and girl. Yellow, meagre, ragged, scowling, wolfish.* But if they were unwilling to even speak with him, what could he possibly do?

He searched for ideas all day Sunday and even lay awake on Sunday night trying to come up with a plan. He and the Good Mischief Team had already tried snooping around the fairgrounds after hours, and all that had done was get then scared off by a ferocious lion. Rabbit had given him some insights, but he also knew that Rabbit wanted him to "figure it out" on his own.

Harry fell asleep feeling burdened. Those two kids would not leave his mind. He could not ever remember feeling so helpless. He dreamed of the children in *A Christmas Carol,* even though it was hardly Christmastime.

93

⠎⠕⠺

The big news in school the following day was how Clive Cantaloni had covered the entire town in his fliers on Sunday. Lots of kids had gone back on Sunday and said the carnival had been awesome. The big top show had been perfect, and the rides had kept heads spinning and stomachs churning. Now more than ever, Harry could not wait to get back. But at the same time, the constant talk about the carnival kept reminding Harry of his failure to find out what the story was with those two strange kids.

It didn't take very long for the two kids to become the topic of conversation when Harry sat down with his buddies at lunch. He'd only been sitting down for a minute or so when Bailey started grilling him.

"You look down, Harry," Bailey said. "What gives?" Bailey's mouth was so full with his peanut butter sandwich that the strawberry jelly was oozing out and sticking to his upper lip.

"Those kids," Harry said. "I can't help but feel like they're in some sort of trouble. And you have jelly all over your mouth, slobby man."

"Ah jeez, those kids again?" Hao said.

Harry shrugged. "I feel bad for them. That's all."

"Well, we did everything we could," Declan said. "That is . . . until that lion scared the snot out of us!"

"Nah, I wasn't scared," Hao said.

"Whatever," Bailey argued. "You screamed the loudest, dude."

The boys laughed about this, but Declan stopped before anyone else. He was looking across the cafeteria with a thoughtful look on his face.

"What is it?" Harry asked.

95

"You know," Declan said. "Maybe we can get some help in finding out a thing or two about those kids."

"Who's going to help?" Harry asked.

Declan pointed behind them. Harry followed his finger, and at first, the only person he saw was Titus Kligore, the mayor's youngest son and, by default, not the closest friend of Harry's. Still, Harry always tried his best with him. Titus was speaking with a group of boys and laughing with a weird sound that was more like an ape than a teenage boy.

"Titus?!" Harry said. "No way!"

"No, not Titus," Declan said. "I meant the guy he's talking to."

"Oh," Harry said, taking another look. "That's Frank Weiller, right?"

"Right. And do you know who his father is?" Declan asked.

"A policeman," Bailey answered.

"That's right," Declan said. "But not just any policeman. Rumor has it that he used to work for the FBI. And even though he's just a cop here in Sleepy Hollow, a lot of people think he's part of a secret task force. Like undercover or something."

"So?" Harry asked. "I mean, that's cool and all, but that doesn't mean Frank can necessarily help."

"I was thinking maybe the acorn doesn't fall too far from the tree," Declan said.

"Yeah," Hao said. "I bet Frank is all into spy gear and everything."

"For sure," Bailey offered. "I heard he has paintball guns and night-vision binoculars. Things like that. If anyone can help you get some answers about those two kids, I bet it's going to be Frank."

"Hmmm," Harry said. He thought it certainly

97

couldn't hurt to look into it. Besides, Frank was a pretty big guy, about the same size as Titus. From the little Harry knew about Frank, he wasn't a bully like Titus. If anything, Frank was quiet and kept to himself most of the time.

"Should we go talk to him?" Hao asked.

Harry frowned. "Maybe later," he said. "I'm not going to go over there while he's talking to Titus."

The boys went back to eating their lunch. From time to time, Harry looked back over at Frank. Near the end of lunch, Frank was sitting by himself. Titus was nowhere to be seen. But just as Harry was about to make his move, the bell rang. Students got up to dump their trays and head to their next class. By the time Harry had thrown his trash away, Frank had disappeared into the crowd.

Without much time to get to class, Harry wasn't able to search for him. But he thought about how cool it would be to go back to the fairgrounds after hours with super-stealthy spy

equipment. And just that fast, Harry started to form a plan.

Once the final bell rang, Harry waited outside of the school. He decided to be by himself, so Frank wouldn't feel like he was being pressured by a team of four kids. Besides, Harry wanted to find out if the rumors were true about Frank before Declan, Bailey, and Hao had a chance to speak with him.

Frank was one of the last kids to come out of school. He walked slowly, with two books tucked under his arm. His large shoulders were slumped, and his brown hair looked as if it might not have seen a brush or comb in a week or so. He walked by himself and looked a little bored. Harry almost felt bad for bothering him when he stepped forward and started walking with him.

"You're Frank Weiller, right?" Harry said.

"Yup. That's me."

"And your dad is Officer Weiller?"

Frank sighed and said, "Yup. Why? Are you in some sort of trouble?"

"No, not really," Harry said. "Look . . . my friends and I are sort of wondering if the rumors about you are true."

100

"What rumors?"

"Well . . . that you're into the same sort of stuff your dad is into. That you have cool spy gear."

Frank suddenly got very serious. He stopped walking and looked at Harry in the same way an adult looked at a kid when there was serious business to discuss. "That might be true," Frank said. "What's it to ya?"

"Well, I have a sort of mystery on my hands and was hoping you'd want to help."

"What kind of a mystery?"

The two boys started walking again as

Harry told him about the carnival and the two kids he had seen. He also told Frank about how he and the Good Mischief Team had tried snooping around the fairgrounds two nights ago only to get scared away by a lion. He then told Frank about his new plan, to go back to the fairgrounds tonight, but this time with some of Frank's spy gear and his knowledge of being stealthy.

Frank seemed interested right away. "That sounds pretty intense," he said. "I'm in. I'd have to sort of sneak out, though. My dad is a cop, you know. He used to work with the FBI. It's pretty hard for me to sneak out. But I think I can manage it."

"So how about we meet around eleven or so tonight?" Harry said.

"I can do that," Frank said. "But I better go for now. I need to go scrounge up dinner somewhere."

"Why do you have to look for dinner?"

Frank shrugged. "Dad works some long hours. He sometimes remembers to leave me money for pizza or Chinese takeout. But sometimes he forgets, like this morning. So I need to figure out what I'm going to have for dinner."

"Why don't you come to my house for supper?" Harry said.

"Really?" Frank asked, clearly surprised.

"Yeah, really. Mom is a great cook, and she always gets excited when I have new kids over from school."

"You're sure it's cool?"

"Absolutely," Harry said. "If you're helping me snoop around Clive Cantaloni's Carnival tonight, the least I can do is invite you over for supper!"

"Gee, thanks," Frank said. "I don't . . . well, I don't usually get invited over to people's houses. I think it's because most kids are freaked out about what my dad does. They think that hanging out with me means my dad will constantly be watching them or something."

"I'm not too worried about that," Harry said. "I'm just really glad to have your help."

Harry and Frank turned down Nightingale Lane, still deep in conversation. Harry had always been good at making new friends, and he was pretty sure he had just made another great one. They talked, they laughed, and more importantly, they made plans for the night's mission.

104

OPERATION BIG TOP

Harry was right. Mary Moon seemed very pleased to have a new face in the house. As Harry and Frank had spent some time playing in the back yard with Harvest, Mary had made a dinner of spaghetti and meatballs, garlic bread, and a salad. When they all sat down to dinner, Harry noticed right away that Frank looked a little uncomfortable. Given what Frank had told Harry about his dad and how he had to often fend for himself for dinner, Harry wondered if Frank wasn't used to big family meals.

"It's certainly nice to have you with us this evening, Frank," Mary Moon said.

"Thanks for having me," Frank said, swirling up a forkful of spaghetti.

106

"I've met your father a few times," John said. "He seems like an awfully busy guy. How is he doing these days?"

"He's good," Frank said. "He's always on the move, working on a case. He still gets calls from the FBI from time to time and . . ."

"Yes?" John asked.

"Sorry," Frank said. "I'm not really supposed to talk about that stuff."

"Ah, I see," John Moon said in a whisper.

"My lips are sealed."

Dinner went well, but Harry kept noticing that Frank would look almost longingly at Mary Moon. Harry didn't know anything about Frank's mother. In fact, he'd never heard anything about her, not at school or even directly from Frank's mouth. But the way Frank looked at Harry's mom, Harry thought that Frank's mother might not be in the picture. This made Harry sad but, at the same time, very glad that he had invited Frank to dinner. No matter what sort of family you came from, everyone deserved the comfort and safety of a big family dinner. In a way, it made Harry feel the same way about Frank as he felt about the two kids at the carnival.

When dinner was over, Harry walked Frank out to the front yard. They stood at the sidewalk for a moment, looking around to make sure there was no one around to eavesdrop.

"Okay," Harry said. "So . . . eleven o' clock at the Pumpkin Patch. Can you make it?"

"That shouldn't be a problem," Frank said.

"And I'll have a lot of gadgets to help find those kids, too."

"Great," Harry said. "And hey. . . I'm glad you could make it for dinner this evening."

"Yeah, me too," Frank said. "You have an awesome family."

Harry smiled and looked back to his house. "Yeah, I know."

Frank nodded but looked a little sad. "Well, see you tonight," he said.

Before Harry could say anything else, Frank had started walking away. Harry watched him go, wishing he had spent a little more time getting to know his new friend.

⌒∿⌒

The shadows of five boys and their bikes stretched out of the Pumpkin Patch at 11:02 that night. The streets were empty, so no one saw them as they sped across Magic Row and toward the looming shapes of the carnival tents. It felt a little strange to Harry to have a fifth member with them but also very exciting.

Harry was so anxious (and nervous, if he was telling the truth) about the mission at hand that he barely even noticed when they passed by Mayor Kligore's house on Folly Farm. He *did* feel a little twinge of fear when the fairground gates came into view. The big top tents reached into the night sky like some old, eerie castle behind them.

Harry knew that Frank had a backpack filled with a few spy gadgets. As for Harry, he had his magic wand tucked securely in his back pocket. It made him feel a bit safer even though he couldn't imagine a scenario where he'd need to use it when it was this late at night and they were investigating the fairgrounds.

This time, the gates were closed and locked. As the boys ditched their bikes and hid them off of the side of the road, it occurred to Harry that what they were about to do was questionable. He was pretty sure this would be considered breaking and entering, or trespassing at least. But he thought of those two kids. If they were lost or being held at the carnival against their will, Harry thought that it was worth taking the risk of getting in trouble

"Who's going first?" Frank asked as he hitched his book bag over his shoulders.

"I'll go first," Harry said. "This was my idea, so I'll take the lead. . . and be the first to get busted if we get caught."

"We won't get caught," Frank said. He reached into his backpack and took out a pair of rad-looking binoculars. He hit a switch on the side, and the lenses glowed with a slight green color.

"Awesome!" Declan exclaimed. "What are those?"

"Night vision binoculars," Frank said.

"Whoa, buddy," Declan said. "Where'd you

110

get those?"

"Ordered them down at the Sleepy Hollow Outfitters."

Harry found this answer a little disappointing. He was thinking he'd maybe gotten them from some military surplus or at least from some trunk hidden under his dad's bed.

Frank put the binoculars to his eyes and then got as close to the gate as he could. He scanned the area, pointing to the left after a few seconds. "Right there," he said. "There's a van with one guy inside. Looks like one of Cantaloni's security guards. But he's snoozing. As long as we're quiet, we should be okay."

111

This made Harry feel a bit better, but not much. He rubbed the sweat from his hands on his pants and then started to climb the big iron gate. It was easier than he thought. The bars were wide and easy to grab. He used his feet to steady himself against the bars as he pulled himself up and climbed. When he reached the top and looked down, he saw that Frank and

Bailey were already on their way up.

Harry scaled down the other side of the gate, and when his feet touched the ground, he knew that there was no turning back now. The ticket booth sat ahead of him, just a murky shape in the darkness. He looked around at all of the shadows as he waited for the others to join him on the ground. He could hear crickets, a stirring wind, and nothing else. The place was totally quiet.

Finally, they were all joined together on the inside of the gate. Harry could see fairly well but really wished he had Frank's night vision goggles. He stopped walking and waved Frank on, letting him take the lead. As Harry fell in behind him, he still recalled the lion that had scared them so badly last time. Even after seeing it do a series of cool tricks at the carnival, Harry still wanted no part of seeing it up close and personal again.

The four members of the Good Mischief Team followed closely behind Frank. While they were all excited and felt like Navy Seals, they were also very scared. Except for Frank . . . he looked like it was Christmas morning. He was having the time of his life as he led his new friends through the dark fairgrounds.

All of a sudden, Frank came to a stop and

held up his hand in a *stop* gesture. Harry and the others froze in their tracks, ducking down behind the cotton candy booth. They huddled together and watched as a man in a red zip-up uniform walked across the lane between the Octopus and the Teacups ride. He was holding a toolbox in his hand and heading to the back of the grounds.

"Probably just a mechanic," Frank whispered. "Working on the rides or something."

They waited for the mechanic to walk out of their sight. When he disappeared behind a series of trucks at the far end of the grounds, the five boys started walking forward again. They walked slow and hunched over just in case they needed to hide again.

"Hey, guys," Bailey said. "Doesn't this make you feel like a soldier?"

"A little," Hao said.

"I feel like we're sneaking through a jungle

or desert or something," Bailey went on. "I feel like . . ." He stopped suddenly. Then, from his mouth came a little *oof* sound.

Harry quickly turned around and saw that Bailey had fallen to the ground. More than that, it looked as if he has snagged his foot on a rope or cord of some kind and then tripped. Harry also saw that the cord was connected to a metal fence surrounding the Octopus ride. Slowly, a section of the fence started to teeter over from the pull of Bailey's weight.

Harry made a quick dash for it, hoping to catch it before it hit the ground and made too much noise. But he wasn't fast enough.

The fence fell over and clattered to the ground. It sounded impossibly loud in the quiet of the night. And to Harry's horror, he saw that the other sections of the fence were also starting to fall in a domino effect behind it. All five sections of the metal fence around the Octopus fell to the ground. Its clattering noise made it impossible to ignore. There was no way it would go unheard by others on the fairgrounds.

Almost right away, they heard a series of footfalls ahead of them.

"It's the mechanic," Frank said, looking through the night vision binoculars. "He's coming back! Our cover has been blown! Abort! Abort!"

All five boys turned on their heels and ran. Harry took a few quick peeks over his shoulder but could not see the mechanic coming after them.

The gate stood right ahead of them. Harry wondered if they would be able to make it over before anyone behind them could catch them. He still saw no one but knew that there was no way the mechanic had not heard the commotion of the falling Octopus fence.

They ran to the fence. Harry was just about to leap onto it when he saw a figure standing there. At first, it looked like a very tall person. But as Harry came to a skidding stop, he saw that there was not one but *two* figures standing there.

"Keep going, Harry!" Declan screamed from behind him.

"I can't," Harry said with fear in his voice. "We've been busted."

117

118

BUSTED

Harry had never been faced with the reality of being in such huge trouble before. He was certain that these figures standing in front of him were the cops. Or maybe it was Clive Cantaloni and some of his security people. Or, worst of all, he wondered if it might be Mayor Kligore.

Yet as he stood there, waiting to be scolded for breaking into the fairgrounds, Harry could actually see the figures standing before him.

At once, his fear washed away. Instead, he felt very confused.

"Honey?" he asked.

His younger sister stood before him, having just come over the gates. She was looking at him like she was trying to figure out a very complicated math problem. Her friend, Claire, stood beside her, looking into the dark with wide eyes.

"Harry? What are *you* doing here?" Honey whispered.

"What are *you* doing here?" Harry asked back.

"Claire and I have come to set the big cats free! And if we couldn't get the cages open, we were going to chain ourselves to them! What about *you?*

"We were trying to find those two kids. We were—"

"I hate to interrupt," Frank said. "But could we maybe settle all of this later? Someone is coming up *right behind us!*"

Just as Frank said this, the entire fairgrounds brightened. Every light in the place came on: the light in the snack booths, the lights surrounding the big tents, and the lights on the rides.

Harry covered his eyes for a moment because it was so bright. The sudden glare of light took them all by surprise

"What are you kids doing here?" a voice said from behind the glare.

Harry's eyes had adjusted enough for him to see that this was the mechanic in the red zip-up uniform. He carried a toolbox in his right hand and looked very upset. Behind him, the security guard that had been asleep got out of his van. He came running over to the group. He looked rather embarrassed to have slept through it all.

"I'm here to save the lions and tigers!" Honey said, stomping her foot like a spoiled three-year-old.

"Save them?" the mechanic asked. "From what?"

"From their imprisonment!"

Harry couldn't help but roll his eyes. Honey was getting carried away now, trying to sound older than she was, and it was making her seem *really* dumb.

"Imprisonment, huh?" the security guard said, finally catching up to the mechanic. "It's funny you should say that. See, I've already called the cops. They'll be here any minute. I don't think they'll take too kindly to a bunch of kids breaking into the carnival grounds after hours."

"Guys, this is no good," Frank said. "My dad is on patrol tonight. If he comes out here and sees what I'm doing, I'll be grounded for *life!*"

Frank started trying to climb the gate, but the security guard shouted right away. "I don't think so! You stay right where you are until the cops get here!"

As if the moment couldn't get any worse, Clive Cantaloni, in his robe and slippers, emerged from the bright lights of the carnival. The great man looked tired, having just been woken up. Harry was amused to see Mr. Cantaloni's parrot perched on the shoulder of his robe. Mr. Cantaloni took in the commotion all around him. Harry watched as several expressions crossed his face: confusion then alarm then anger.

123

"And just what is going on here?" Clive Cantaloni asked. He pushed his long mane of white hair back from his face.

"We caught these boys breaking in and then trying to escape," the mechanic said. "And then these girls were just now breaking in."

"Is that so?" Mr. Cantaloni asked.

"Yes, sir," said the mechanic. "I've already called the police."

"Good, good." Mr. Cantaloni approached the seven kids and gave them a stern look—the sort of look that was usually saved only for angry parents and principals. When his eyes landed on Harry, he paused and frowned.

"You look familiar," he said. "How do I know you?"

"Well, I," Harry started.

But then Mr. Cantaloni snapped his fingers, interrupting Harry. "I remember now. You were the kid that came on Friday afternoon to ask for a spot in my magic show!"

Harry nodded, looking at the ground in embarrassment. In the distance, Harry heard cars approaching. He looked to the other side of the iron gate and could see headlights drawing closer. As they neared, he could see that these were the cops the mechanic had called.

124

"Harry," Honey said, suddenly coming to his side. "This is bad, huh?"

"Yeah," Harry said, taking her hand in his. "We're in pretty bad trouble here."

As the cop cars pulled up to the gate, the security guard opened it to let the cars in. Their headlights washed across the fairground, adding to the already frantic lights. As the cars parked, Harry saw something over near the Bottle Toss. There were two shadows, dashing behind another booth. The shadows looked small, human-like, and as if they were holding hands.

Harry started forward but was stopped by a forceful voice.

"Stay where you are, young man," said one of the cops as they stepped out of the car. Two cars had shown up, and four officers were coming toward Harry, the Good Mischief Team, Honey, Claire, and Frank. Clive Cantaloni watched it all, standing shoulder to shoulder in his robe and slippers with the security guard and the mechanic.

It was getting out of hand way too fast. Harry tried to imagine what his parents were going to say. He looked to Honey and wondered if she had ever *really* been punished before. If not, this little stunt would likely be her first real offense.

"Frank!" one of the cops said. The cop came walking over quickly and stood directly in front of Frank. "What are you *doing?*"

"Sorry, Dad," he said. "I was just trying to help my new friends."

"Friends?" Officer Weiller said. "I've never seen them before."

"I sort of just met them."

"And you're breaking the law with them?"

"It's not like that, Dad. It's just that—"

Another car was approaching the gates now. Another set of headlights turned into the entrance and came through the open gate.

Harry watched the car with terrified eyes and was pretty sure the arrival of this car meant that his life was over.

He knew the car very well. It belonged to his mother.

"That's Mom," Honey whispered from beside him.

"Yeah," Harry said.

He could see his mother's face through the windshield. Somehow the look of disappointment on her face was worse than any punishment she could ever give.

"Harry Moon and Honey Moon!"

Mary Moon got out of her car and walked toward the group of people that stood near the gate. When she arrived, she did so with more authority than the security guard or the cops. Even the cops seemed to notice her attitude, backing up a step to let her have a word with her children. Harry noticed that Officer Weiller stayed by Frank, a hand on his shoulder and a scowl on his face.

"Sorry, Mom," Honey said, close to tears.

"What is the *meaning* of this?" Mary shouted. She looked at Honey and shook her head. "You're lousy at sneaking out. I heard you when you left and followed you here. I expect this sort of nonsense out of your brother from time to time, but not you! Honey, what were you thinking?"

"I just wanted to save the big cats!"

Harry could tell that she was on the verge of *really* crying. He, on the other hand, was too scared to cry. He had never seen his mother so upset . . . so *furious.*

"I'm sorry, Mom," he said.

"What are you doing here, Harry?" she asked, trying to remain calm.

"The two kids . . ."

He tried to explain, and as he did, everyone else seemed to start talking at the same time. The scene became a blur of voices as Officer Weiller started asking Frank tons of questions, and the cops and security guard started inter- rogating Bailey, Declan, Hao, and Claire.

"If you were so worried about those kids," Mary said through the noise, "you should have been more direct with your dad and me. We could have called the authorities or helped you figure it out. But trespassing, Harry! This is serious business!"

"I know," he said. "I'm so sorry."

Mary opened her mouth to say something else. But, just like everyone else that had tried speaking in the last five minutes or so, she was cut off.

Clive Cantaloni stood on the platform of the Test Your Strength contraption. He looked out at all of them. His gruff voice was so thick and loud that Harry thought it sounded like thunder.

"Excuse me, please, everyone," he said. "If I might have a word?"

Slowly, the clamor and commotion between the police, the kids, and Mr. Cantaloni's employees died down. Everyone turned and stared at him. Harry, meanwhile, looked back at the area where he had seen the two shadows. He nudged Frank and pointed to the night vision binoculars that Frank still wore around his neck. Frank handed them over. Harry brought them to his eyes.

Looking through the binoculars, everything

had a soft green glow to it. Harry had seen something like this in movies but had never seen anything like it in real life. It was cool in a sort of creepy way. He scanned the fairgrounds and spotted the two kids. They were hunkered down behind a hot dog vendor booth, watching as things unfolded. The little girl looked scared as usual, but the boy was watching everything very closely.

As Harry looked at them through the night vision binoculars, he was dimly aware that Mr. Cantaloni was beginning to speak from the Test Your Strength platform.

131

"Settle down, please," he said. His thunderous voice grew into soft authority, a tone that made it impossible to tell if he was about to yell at everyone or have a polite conversation.

"I appreciate the hard work of my employees and the Sleepy Hollow police," Mr. Cantaloni said. "But as this is currently my place of business, I would like to give each of these youngsters a chance to explain themselves before serious actions are taken."

He then cast Harry a very nasty stare and added, "I know I'd love to hear what they have to say."

Perhaps because Mr. Cantaloni was looking at him, every other set of eyes also turned in Harry's direction. He was still holding the night vision binoculars in his hands. He handed them back to Frank as he slowly stepped forward toward the Test Your Strength game. As he made his way to Mr. Cantaloni's side, he looked at the hot dog booth and thought he could still see the murky shapes of the two kids hiding in the shadows.

I can help them now, Harry thought. *I've gotten myself into a whole heap of trouble, but at least I can help those kids now.*

He turned around and looked at the gathered crowd. His mother was gazing at him with disappointment on her face. "Son," Officer Weiller said, "I hope you have a darn good explanation for what you've done tonight."

Harry glanced back over at the hot dog stand and nodded. "Yes, sir. I do."

THE BOY AND THE GIRL

"Officer Weiller, none of this was Frank's idea," Harry explained. "I sort of recruited him earlier today. He's here because I asked him to come along. So please don't take it too hard on him. Even though he was helping me with something that wasn't totally honest, he was really brave."

Officer Weiller looked down at Frank with a frown, but some of his anger seemed to have vanished.

"And Mr. Cantaloni, I promise you that we weren't here to do anything wrong. We aren't those kinds of kids."

"I don't care *what* kind of kids you are," Mr. Cantaloni said. "This is trespassing. And after the fire on Saturday, I can take no chances with security. So unless you have a very good reason for being here, I'm afraid I'll have to press charges against your family. I certainly hope this has nothing to do with me turning down your offer to perform at the magic show."

"No, sir," Harry said. "Not at all. You see . . . when I was here Friday and walking back out of the gates, I saw these two kids. They looked really scared. They looked like they were lost. One of them was crying, and when I asked them if they needed help, they sort of freaked out. It was clear they didn't want me around."

"Hold on," one of the cops said. "Two kids were here without an adult before the carnival even opened?"

"I'm pretty sure," Harry said.

"Can you prove it?" Officer Weiller said.

"Well, ask them for yourself," Harry said. "I'm certain they're hiding behind the hot dog stand."

All eyes turned in that direction. Officer Weiller even took Frank's night vision goggles and grabbed a peek. Slowly, the cops started walking toward the hot dog stand. They walked slowly, and it was clear that they had spotted the kids within a few seconds. One of the cops was a woman, and she hunkered down and extended a hand.

"Come on out," she said. "It's okay. We just want to help."

As Harry watched, the boy did come out of his hiding spot behind the hot dog stand. He looked around at the gathered crowd, and his eyes finally landed on Harry. The boy gave him a very brief smile and then looked back at the cops. He took another step and then another. He looked back at the girl, but she was not following him.

Harry caught sight of her, backing away farther into the shadows. The boy seemed confused, reaching out to her and gesturing for her to come with him. She shook her head and went running away instead.

"Little girl!" one of the cops said. "Please come back."

But the girl was not interested in coming back. She was far too scared. And she was quick too. She had already run behind the Octopus, toward the back of the fairgrounds. As she ran away, Officer Weiller went to the boy's side. "Are you okay?" he asked the boy.

"Yes. But Sue is . . . well, she's scared. She's so scared of everything and . . ."

136

At that moment, the grounds were filled with a loud and terrible roar. It was a roar that Harry and the Good Mischief Team knew well; it was the roar of the lion that had nearly had them for dinner a few nights ago.

"Oh no," Mr. Cantaloni said. "She's made it to the stables! The tigers and my lion will be spooked by her."

Without a word, everyone went running in the same direction the little girl had run to. Within seconds, Harry saw why the lion was roaring. The little girl—Sue, the boy had called her—was climbing up the side of the large barn that held all of the animals. She was climbing up a ladder that led to the roof. The lion was standing on its back legs, swatting at the front of the barn, trying to get to her.

"Bernard, *no!*" Mr. Cantaloni demanded.

The lion turned to Mr. Cantaloni and seemed very confused. He gave one final roar and swatted at the barn one more time. It was a very strong swat, causing the barn to shake a bit. Fifteen feet above their heads, Sue looked down at them. She looked at the boy she had been hiding with and let out a weak, little cry.

She reached up for the next rung on the ladder as she looked at the boy, but her hand missed the rung. She slipped, her feet coming off of the ladder. For a terrifying moment, she hung by just one hand and then the strength in her fingers gave out. She dropped from the ladder and started to fall.

138

While she was fortunate enough to not be descending into the lion's den, she was still falling from a nasty height. She could break an arm or a leg or much worse.

Everyone in the crowd let out a gasp. Harry gasped, perhaps loudest of all, but he also *acted*.

He pulled his wand from his back pocket and pointed it directly beneath Sue. He did it without even thinking about it, just acting in the hopes of saving her life or, at the very least, preventing a broken bone or two.

"ABRACADABRA!" he shouted.

There was a flash of color along the ground just beneath her. A split second before Sue made contact with the ground, an enormous pile of cotton candy appeared. Sue fell into this soft, pink cloud. There was a funny *floof* sort of sound as she hit it. From what Harry could tell, she had not hit the ground at all. The cotton

candy cloud had totally cushioned her fall.

Two of the cops and the boy immediately ran to her. The boy started digging through the fluffy candy to reach Sue.

Meanwhile, everyone else looked at Harry in incredulity. This included Clive Cantaloni, who stared at Harry with his mouth opened wide in disbelief.

140

Harry did not allow himself time to bask in their appreciation, though. He ran over to the huge mound of pink with the rest of the Good Mischief Team (and Frank) at his heels. He got there just as the boy was pulling Sue out of the cotton candy.

It was all in her hair and smudged on her face. Strangely enough, though, Sue was smiling. She embraced her brother and then looked directly at Harry.

"Thank you," she said with a shy voice.

"Sure," Harry said. "Are you okay?"

She looked at the gathered crowd. It was clear that she was uncomfortable, but she nodded.

Clive Cantaloni came rushing up to Harry. His mouth was still open in awe, and his eyes were wide with shock. "Young man, how did you do that?"

Harry could only shrug. He was never really comfortable talking about the Deep Magic . . . especially with people he didn't know all that well.

"Have you always been able to <u>do</u> those sorts of things?" Mr. Cantaloni asked.

Harry wasn't sure how to answer. Fortunately for him, he had a group of great friends that sometimes did the talking for him.

"Are you kidding?" Hao said. "Harry's the best."

"Harry is amazing," Declan said. "You made a huge mistake not having him join your magic show!"

"That's for sure," Mr. Cantaloni said.

"Wait, wait, hold on now," Officer Weiller said. Although it was clear that he was impressed by what Harry had done, he was still trying to remain professional. "We still need to find out who these kids belong to. Mr. Cantaloni, do you have underage children working as part of your carnival?"

142

"Goodness, no! In fact, I have never seen these children before! I'm just as shocked and surprised as you are."

All four of the cops looked at Mr. Cantaloni with suspicion in their eyes. The lady officer turned to Sue and her brother and asked, "Why are you here? Where are your parents?"

The two kids looked at one another without saying a word. After a few moments, the boy shrugged and then sighed. He began to tell

their story, and as he did, the entire crowd was once again stunned to silence.

The boy's name was Jeff, and the girl's name was Sue. Harry had been right in assuming they were brother and sister. Sue was eight, and Jeff was eleven. When Jeff told their story, Sue stayed by his side the whole time.

143

"I know it might get us into some trouble," Jeff said, "but Sue and I are runaways. We were both living with this foster family that was never there. Sometimes, they were really mean to Sue. One day, I was reading her a book about circus animals, and she thought it would be cool to see a real live elephant. And I had always wanted to be one of those guys that walks the tightrope . . . or an acrobat, you know? But I knew there was no way we'd ever see any of that in real life. But then things got really bad with the foster family, and one night I woke Sue up and we snuck out. That was about three weeks ago. And on that same night, we saw a poster for Clive Cantaloni's Carnival and Magic Show. We *just* missed it in the town we were living in, but I saw on the poster that it was coming to Sleepy Hollow. So we came here and have been hiding out ever since Mr. Cantaloni started setting things up."

As he wrapped things up, Harry watched as one of the policemen turned away from the crowd. He pulled out a fancy-looking walkie-talkie and started speaking with someone. The only words Harry heard clearly were children, endangered, and social worker.

"You're right," Officer Weiller said. "You *could* get into trouble for running away like that. But if you can tell us about this foster family, we can look into it."

"Don't make us go back," Sue pleaded.

"If you're right about this family not being good to you, we won't," another officer said. "But for now, just stick with us. We'll make sure you stay safe."

"Okay, thanks," Jeff said.

"Yes, thank you," Sue echoed.

A brief silence filled the night. A faint sound of chewing was the only thing that could be heard. Harry looked in the direction of the sound and couldn't help but smile when he saw that Honey, Claire, Declan, Bailey, and Hao were all eating from the gigantic pile of cotton candy that had saved Sue's fall.

145

Mr. Cantaloni hunkered down on his knees in front of Jeff and Sue. Any traces of anger that had been on his face earlier were gone. "So you two have been hiding around here for all this time?" he asked.

"We're awful sorry," Jeff said.

"Have you been eating?"

"Pizza scraps, leftover hot dogs, even some bone meal," Jeff said, hanging his head in embarrassment.

"We'll get you a proper meal," Mr. Cantaloni said. "But I must ask . . . have you seen my real live elephant, Flo?"

Sue's eyes lit up, and she nodded furiously.

"Have you actually got to *meet* her?" Mr. Cantaloni asked.

"No," Sue said.

"Well, let's fix that right now, shall we?" he said. He looked back at the policemen and asked, "Would that be alright?"

"Only if I get to meet her too," Officer Weiller said with a smile.

"Of course!"

Harry watched them walk to the back of the big barn, and within seconds he heard the trumpeting sounds of Flo greeting them. Harry was humbled to know that he had judged Clive Cantaloni unfairly. Cantaloni was proving that it was dangerous to judge someone before you got to know them. and even then it wasn't a good idea.

As he thought about this, a hand landed on his shoulder. He turned to see his mom and the tired look she wore.

"You did a fine thing by saving that girl from her fall," Mary Moon said. "But we're going to get you home now. It's a school day tomorrow, and after that, you better believe we have a punishment to dole out."

147

"Yes, ma'am," Harry said.

"You, too, Honey," Mary said. "Don't think I've forgotten about you."

"Yes, ma'am."

"Declan, Bailey, Hao, and Claire, you come along, too. I'm going to call each of your parents and then pray that they are forgiving."

"Yes, ma'am," they said in unison.

With that, the Moon family made their exit from the grounds of Clive Cantaloni's Carnival and Magic Show. As Harry picked up his bike from its hiding spot on the other side of the road, he heard Flo's trumpet-like voice again. Harry imagined Sue petting Flo's trunk, and despite the trouble he was in, couldn't help but smile.

148

JOINING THE CIRCUS

Harry had been sure that the night he'd saved Sue's life with cotton candy would be the last time he would ever be allowed to step foot on the fairgrounds. But because his mother had extended such huge grace upon him, Harry found himself there again on Thursday night. More than that, he found himself sweating nervously behind the large, red tent in the center of the fairgrounds.

Clive Cantaloni was standing beside him, looking at Harry with a huge smile. "Are you ready?" he asked.

"I think so," Harry answered.

"It may seem like a lot of people," Clive said. "But don't let that bother you. I know some people say to imagine a crowd in their underwear, but that never worked for me. I always prefer to imagine them wearing duck costumes. Give that a try."

150

"I will," Harry said. "Thanks."

As he waited for his call to enter the big, red tent, he thought about how crazy the last few days had been. Frank had passed on information he'd gotten from his father to Harry and the Good Mischief Team. As it turned out, the foster parents Jeff and Sue had run away from were indeed problematic. That meant that Jeff and Sue would have to find a new foster home . . . something that Clive Cantaloni himself volunteered for. There was apparently a ton of paperwork to be done and some sort of

training, but he was actively working toward becoming a foster parent for Jeff and Sue.

And then, yesterday, Mary Moon had taken a phone call just before dinner. She had come to Harry's room and told him that although he was still grounded, there was someone on the phone with an opportunity that she could not let him miss out on. Harry took the call and spoke with Mr. Cantaloni for about five minutes.

151

He gave Harry a fifteen-minute spot during the magic show. Not only that, but it was to be the closing act on the last night of the carnival. After tonight's show, Clive Cantaloni's Carnival and Magic Show would be leaving Sleepy Hollow and moving on to Orlando, Florida. But as Harry understood it, Clive Cantaloni would be staying in town until the foster parenting process was wrapped up and he could legally call Jeff and Sue part of his family.

All of this replayed through Harry's head as Clive went into the tent to start the show.

Within moments, Harry heard calliope music starting up and then Clive Cantaloni's voice through the speakers. The show began. The animal parade entered the ring. Harry went through his act in his mind, trying to make sure he was ready to be able to give it his absolute best.

"You seem nervous," said a friendly voice from behind him.

He turned to see Rabbit standing there. Harry wasn't too surprised to see him munching on a candied apple.

"I *am* nervous, Rabbit," Harry said. "There's a *lot* of people in there!"

"And?"

"And I've never performed for that many people!"

"Harry, do you recall the cotton candy trick you did the other night? The one that saved Sue?"

"Yes."

"You did that without much of a thought. It came naturally to you, right?"

"Right."

"That's the sign of not only a great magician but of someone that has a heart for others. As I told you, everyone needs a little help from time to time . . . and that includes even you. So here I am to do that. I am here to remind you that whenever you seek it, there it will be. The Deep Magic."

153

Harry nodded. "Thanks, Rabbit."

"Anytime," Rabbit said through a mouthful of candied apple.

Harry continued to wait . . . and wait some more. Clive announced the trapeze and high-wire act. The butterflies inside Harry leapt in anticipation. Harry would be up next. He did his best to remember that the Good Magic within was enough to overcome any of his nervousness. He waited and waited as the crowd gasped and cheered. This was it. This was the big time. This was the big top.

As he stood outside the ring at the back of the tent, Harry noticed the curtain being untied. The backstage curtain parted. To his surprise, Bailey, Declan, and Hao came walking in. "What are you guys doing?" Harry asked in disbelief.

"Getting you into a huddle," said Bailey. Harry knew exactly what that meant, but he was also aware that the trapeze act, which he had seen many times, was almost finished.

"Do we have the time?" asked Harry, nervously.

"Of course we have the time!" answered Hao. He put his arm over Harry's shoulder. Harry smiled.

Bailey ushered the guys together. They put their arms over one another's shoulders.

"I wonder if this anthem will survive our high school days?" asked Hao.

Whether or not the song would, it stood for their friendship *now*. Harry was happy and honored to have such good friends with him in middle school. So they huddled and spoke softly, encouraging Harry.

We don't fight with sticks and stones
We don't want to break your bones
We have a much more ingenious scheme
We are the Good Mischief Team!

Might does not make right,
So when we take on the epic fight
We are trained to follow the gleam
We are the Good Mischief Team!

We never like to make things tragic
We use reason, heart, and magic
We take the lead from the brightest dream
For we are the Good Mischief Team!

"Thanks, guys," Harry said. Their anthem had its own magic. Harry was now pumped.

His nervousness had faded away. And it was perfect timing too. For at the side of the ring, Harry heard Clive Cantaloni introducing him.

". . . and without further ado," Clive Cantaloni said in his powerful, gruff voice, "I give you Sleepy Hollow's very own *Harry Moon!*"

As Harry stepped into the tent, the applause was epic.

156

He had never heard the roar of a thousand hands applauding before. He was sure he was very red in the face as a spike of embarrassment passed through him. Mr. Cantaloni had given him some showman tips on the phone the night before, and Harry did his best to follow some of them. First, he made sure he was smiling before he looked at the audience in a friendly way. Then he started talking, but not too much. It was a trick of the trade . . . to talk to the crowd just enough to keep them laughing and in a good mood. He knew this from the shows he had performed, but it was always nice to remember it, especially with the biggest crowd he had ever known.

For the next fifteen minutes, Harry did some of his favorite tricks. He pulled out the scarves. He fiddled with some hat tricks. He got some laughs. Some applause. When his top hat was loaded with fruit, he shook it, turned it upside down, and gave it a loud "ABRACADABRA" with his wand. When he lifted the hat, there was a fruit smoothie in a glass hiding underneath the stool.

Then the tall clown on stilts came to the center of the ring and pulled the stool away. Now, Harry Moon stood alone with just his wand, his hat, and his invisible rabbit.

After he had shown the crowd that his hat was empty again, he placed it in the center of the ring. He was getting ready for his finale. He was planning to wind it up with a bang. A sole spotlight shone on the brim of the black top hat. With another "ABRACADABRA," Harry ran his wand over the open hat.

With the hat on the ground, Harry bent down and reached his right hand into it. He pulled and pulled and pulled. He looked out at the audience and wiped his brow as if he were sweating. They laughed. He reached his hand in again. He yanked and yanked and yanked. This time a white paw emerged. Then, the paw disappeared just as quickly. The crowd moaned in a feigned dismay.

Harry stood up and turned to the audience. It was all in good fun. "My rabbit can be shy," he said to the crowd. "But if you will help coax him, he'll come out. He just needs a little encouragement. So I'll pull and then, as one, we will shout *ABRACADABRA*, and *together*, we'll get him outta my hat. Are you with me on this?"

"Yes," the crowd shouted.

"I can't hear you. Are you with me on this?" Harry asked again.

"YES!"

This time the crowd roared.

"That's better!" Harry said with a smile. "Now, as I pull on Mister Shy, on three, you shout ABRACADABRA." Harry planted his two shiny, black dress shoes in an exaggerated fashion into the ground. He understood that this was a massive arena. He needed to make his gestures bigger so the audience could see them from the highest bleacher seats.

He rubbed his hands like a laborer on an oil rig ready to go to work. The audience laughed. He acted as if he was putting all his back muscle into the feat as he hunched his back and gave his spine a wiggle. The audience was with him for they laughed again at his antics.

Knowing he had the crowd, Harry reached into the hat with both of his hands and counted with the audience. "ONE . . . TWO . . . THREE!"

Harry pulled. The audience shouted, "ABRACADABRA!"

160

The spotlight burned hot as Harry pulled the largest rabbit the audience had ever seen from the hat. Harry had the great black-and-white rabbit by both paws. Clearly, the rabbit was heavy. He gently dropped the rabbit to the ground.

Acting "shy," Rabbit stood up in the center of the ring. He was three times the size of the top hat! He came up to Harry's waist! The audience *oohed* and *ahhed* at the sight of Rabbit's massive size.

Harry continued to play with the audience. With some coaxing, Rabbit demonstrated his marvelous abilities. When the finale grew to its crescendo, the audience was on its feet.

161

"You know, my friends," Harry said, "from time to time, we all need a little help. So keep your hands together and let's encourage Rabbit to reach for the moon." Of course, Harry was echoing what Rabbit had told him just days earlier.

By this time, the audience was enthralled. Harry shouted, "Fly! Fly! Fly!"

The audience applauded and shouted along with him. Rabbit stood in the center of the ring. His black-and-white face, like a clown mask shining from beneath the spotlight, seemed to smile with all the motivation.

The people in the audience lifted their eyes as Rabbit rose silently from the ring. Like an untethered helium balloon, Rabbit floated gently, effortlessly. Once he reached the peak of the big top, he turned his face to the audience. There was that smile again. He sailed across the fabric of the tent as the lights brightened.

162

They watched Rabbit glide in the air, but in their hearts, everyone could sense they were watching something other than a rabbit flying. The fur of Rabbit expanded as he sailed, growing into a great silver cloud. At the top of his flight, as Rabbit fell from the ceiling above the audience, he broke apart into snowy particles. The tent was filled with the gentle flurry of wonder.

As Rabbit dropped like snowflakes, the audience's eyes were redirected by the spinning trajectory of the snowfall back toward the stage. It was snowing everywhere, even upon Harry. The crowd went quiet in the power of this marvel. Like the first snow on warm soil, the flakes did not stick. This snowfall simply vanished into thin air.

"Thank you, everyone!" said Harry. "May the magic never leave you!"

Instantly, the tent was filled with the joyous sounds of Flo's trumpet-like sounds and thunderous applause. She came marching out onto the floor. Sitting on her back was Clive Cantaloni. Sitting in front of Mr. Cantaloni were Sue and Jeff.

163

Harry looked up at Sue and Jeff and gave them a smile. They returned it and somehow, even through the constant cheering from the crowd, Sue's laughter from the back of the elephant meant the most to Harry.

It was easily one of the best moments of Harry Moon's young life.

164

ONE LAST TRICK

The next morning, on his way to school, Harry noticed that the tents in the distant horizon were gone. The carnival was no longer in town although Clive Cantaloni was sticking around to see what he could do about becoming a foster parent for Jeff and Sue. Harry was on his usual route to school, where he would meet Declan, Bailey, and Hao two blocks away.

He was not alone, though. Rabbit walked along beside him. Rabbit was quiet but kept looking at Harry with thoughtful eyes. Harry knew this look; it meant that Rabbit had something to say but was waiting for the right time to say it.

"I have to admit," Rabbit finally said, "your magic show last night was exceptional."

"Thanks," Harry replied.

"And the discipline your parents gave you for breaking into the fairgrounds . . . have you come to terms with it? Do you understand why they were so strict?"

Harry thought about it for a moment. He was grounded for two weeks. His parents had taken away all video games and other electronics for two weeks. Also, he was not able to hang with his friends after school during that time. Harry thought it was a bit harsh, given what his trespassing had produced, the discovery of the two kids and the possibility of a new foster home for them.

"I guess," he said. "I know the trespassing was wrong, but then I look at all the good it caused and . . . well, it seems a little unfair."

"Remember, Harry . . . you *knew* you were breaking the law. You knew you'd get in trouble if you were found out. And when you got caught, that made you feel guilty, right?"

"And embarrassed."

Rabbit put his arm around his friend as they continued to move down the sidewalk. "Harry?"

"Yes, Rabbit?"

"You're meeting with Clive Cantaloni once you're no longer grounded?"

"Yes. He asked me to teach him some of my magic."

"And you've agreed to it?" Rabbit asked.

"I'll show him a few tricks and tell him

about the Deep Magic."

"Great," Rabbit replied. "I wonder, though . . . do you think you could manage to see if he has any candied apples left over from the carnival?"

Harry laughed. "Sure enough."

With that, Rabbit was gone. Ahead, Harry saw the Good Mischief Team waiting for him to finish their walk to school.

168

"Hi, Harry," Declan said. "How goes the grounding?"

"Ah, you know," Harry shrugged.

"So how are you holding up, Harry?"

Harry thought of Sue smiling at him as she sat on the back of Flo.

"Me?" Harry asked. "I'm doing just great."

170

BE SURE TO READ THE CONTINUING AND
AMAZING ADVENTURES OF HARRY MOON

MARK ANDREW POE

The Adventures of Harry Moon author, Mark Andrew Poe, never thought about being a children's writer growing up. His dream was to love and care for animals, specifically his friends in the rabbit community.

Along the way, Mark became successful in all sorts of interesting careers. He entered the print and publishing world as a young man and his company did really, really well.

Mark became a popular and nationally

sought-after health care advocate for the care and well-being of rabbits.

Years ago, Mark came up with the idea of a story about a young man with a special connection to a world of magic, all revealed through a remarkable rabbit friend. Mark worked on his idea for several years before building a collaborative creative team to help bring his idea to life. And Harry Moon was born.

In 2014, Mark began a multi-book print series project intended to launch *The Adventures of Harry Moon* into the youth marketplace as a hero defined by a love for a magic where love and 'DO NO EVIL' live. Today, Mark continues to work on the many stories of Harry Moon. He lives in suburban Chicago with his wife and his 25 rabbits.

The AMAZING Adventures Of

HARRY MOON

Wand - Paper - Scissors

Inspired by true events   Mark Andrew Poe

HARRY MOON is up to his eyeballs in magic in the small town of Sleepy Hollow. His arch enemy, Titus Kligore, has eyes on winning the Annual Scary Talent Show. Harry has a tough job ahead if he is going to steal the crown. He takes a chance on a magical rabbit who introduces him to the deep magic. Harry decides the best way forward is to DO NO EVIL— and the struggle to defeat Titus while winning the affection of the love of his life goes epic.

EVERYONE IS TALKING ABOUT THE ADVENTURES OF HARRY MOON

"After making successful Disney movies like ALADDIN and LITTLE MERMAID, I could never figure out where the magic came from. Now I know. Harry Moon had it all along."

David Kirkpatrick
Former Production Chief, Walt Disney Studios

"This may well be one of the most important kid's series in a long time."

- Paul Lewis,
Founder,
Family University
Foundation

"Come on. His name is Harry Moon. How do I not read this?"

- Declan Black
Kid, age 13

"A great coming-of-age book with life principals. Harry Moon is better than Goosebumps and Wimpy Kid. Who'da thunk it?

- Michelle Borquez
Author and Mom

THE

AMAZING
ADVENTURES OF

HARRY MOON

TIME MACHINE

Inspired by true events   Mark Andrew Poe

The irrepressible magician of Sleepy Hollow, Harry Moon, sets about to speed up time. Overnight, through some very questionable magic, Harry wishes himself into becoming the high school senior of his dreams. Little did he know that by unleashing time, Harry Moon would come face-to-face with the monster of his worst nightmare. Will Harry find his way home from this supernatural mess?

EVERYONE IS TALKING ABOUT THE ADVENTURES OF HARRY MOON

"Friendship, forgiveness and adventure - Harry Moon will entertain kids and parents alike. My children will have every book in this series on their bookshelf as my gift to them!"

– Regina Jennings
Author and Mom

"Magical and stupendously inspirational, Harry Moon is a hero for the 21st century tween. I wish I had Harry at DISNEY!"

David Kirkpatrick
Former Production Chief, Walt Disney Studios

I can't wait for my next book. Where is the Harry Moon video game?

- Jackson Maison
Kid - age 12

I love my grandchildren and I love Harry Moon. I can't wait to introduce the kids to someone their own age who values life like I do. I hope Harry Moon never ends.

– Scott Hanson
Executive Director, Serve West Dallas and grandpa

$14.99
ISBN 978-1-943785-04-9
51499>

THE AMAZING ADVENTURES OF
HARRY MOON

HALLOWEEN NIGHTMARES

Inspired by true events   Mark Andrew Poe

While other kids are out trick-or-treating, eighth-grade magician Harry Moon is flying on a magic cloak named Impenetrable. Harry and Rabbit speed past severed hands, boiling cauldrons and graveyard witching rituals on their way to unravel a decade old curse at the annual Sleepy Hollow Halloween Bonfire. The sinister Mayor Kligore and Oink are in for the fight of their lives.

EVERYONE IS TALKING ABOUT THE ADVENTURES OF HARRY MOON

"When a character like Harry Moon comes along, you see how important a great story can be to a kid growing up."

- Susan Dawson, Middle School Teacher

"Harry Moon is one wildly magical ride. After making successful films like ALADDIN and LITTLE MERMAID, I wondered where the next hero was coming from Harry Moon has arrived!"

David Kirkpatrick
Former Production Chief, Walt Disney Studios

"This is a book I WANT to read."

- Bailey Black
13-Year Old Kid

"A hero with guts who champions truth in the face of great danger. I wish I was thirteen again! If you work with kids, pay attention to Harry Moon."

- Ryan Frank, a Dad and President, KidzMatter

THE
AMAZING
ADVENTURES OF
HARRY MOON

THE SCARY SMART HOUSE

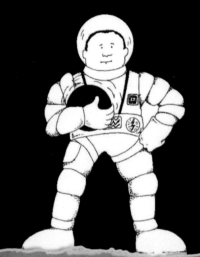

Inspired by true events   Mark Andrew Poe

When Harry's sister wins a national essay contest in technology, the whole Moon family is treated to a dream weekend in the ultimate, fully loaded, smart house designed by Marvel Modbot, the Walt Disney of the 21st century. It's an incredible blast, with driverless cars and a virtual reality world. That is, until evil thinking invades the smart technology running the smart house, turning that dream tech weekend into an nightmare! The Moons look to Harry and Rabbit to stop the evil before its too late.

EVERYONE IS TALKING ABOUT THE ADVENTURES OF HARRY MOON

"The Moon family's smart house takes on a bone-tingling dimension when the technology that runs it appears haunted. Say hello to SECOS -a scary Smart Evil Central Operating System!" –David Kirkpatrick, Former Production Chief, Walt Disney Studios

"I'm a grandpa and Harry Moon is a throw-back to the good old days when kids took on wrong and wrestled it to the ground. My grandkids are getting every book."
– Mark Janes, English and Drama Teacher, Grandfather

"If I was stranded on a desert island, I would want a mat, a pillow, a Harry Moon book and a hatchet"
- Charley, KID, age 11

"I pride myself on never making a bad shot. I focus on perfect form and being rock steady. Like me, Harry Moon delivers under pressure. This kid's my hero."
– Jim Burnworth, Extreme Archer, The Outdoor Channel

$14.99 US / $22.50 CAN
ISBN 978-1-943785-30-8

THE
AMAZING
ADVENTURES OF

HARRY MOON

HAUNTED PIZZA

SLEEPY HOLLOW SLICE

Inspired by true events   Mark Andrew Poe

The new Pizza Slice is doing booming business, but the kids in Sleepy Hollow Middle School are transforming into strange creatures the more they eat of the haunted cheesy delicacy. Even the Good Mischief Team are falling under the spell of the new haunted pizza slices, putting Harry and his magic Rabbit on the scent to the truth behind the peperoni mystery.

EVERYONE IS TALKING ABOUT THE ADVENTURES OF HARRY MOON

"The Moon family's smart house takes on a bone-tingling dimension when the technology that runs it appears haunted. Say hello to SECOS -a scary Smart Evil Central Operating System!" –David Kirkpatrick, Former Production Chief, Walt Disney Studios

"I'm a grandpa and Harry Moon is a throw-back to the good old days when kids took on wrong and wrestled it to the ground. My grandkids are getting every book."
- Mark Janes, English and Drama Teacher, Grandfather

"If I was stranded on a desert island, I would want a mat, a pillow, a Harry Moon book and a hatchet"
- Charley, KID, age 11

"I pride myself on never making a bad shot. I focus on perfect form and being rock steady. Like me, Harry Moon delivers under pressure. This kid's my hero."
- Jim Burnworth, Extreme Archer, The Outdoor Channel

$14.99 US / $22.50 CAN
ISBN 978-1-943785-38-4
90000>
9 781943 785384

THE ENCHANTED WORLD OF HONEY MOON

MOUNTAIN MAYHEM

Suzanne Brooks Kuhn   Created by Mark Andrew Poe

Hit the trail girls! It's on to the Appalachian Trail. Honey and the Spooky Scouts set off on a mountain trek to earn their final Mummy Mates patch. But an inept troop leader, a flash flood and a campfire catastrophe threaten to keep them from reaching the Sleepy Hollow finish line in time. When all seems lost, Honey Moon takes charge and nothing will stop her from that final patch!

"Honey is a bit of magical beauty...adventure and brains rolled into one."
David Kirkpatrick, Former Production Chief, Walt Disney Studios

"Magic, mystery and a little mayhem. Three things that make a story great. Honey Moon is a great story."
-- Dawn Moore
Life Coach and Educator

"A wonderful experience for girls looking for a new hero. I think her name is Honey Moon." - Nancy Dimes, Teacher & Mom

"I absolutely cannot wait to begin my next adventure with Honey Moon. I love her"
– Carly Wujcik, Kid, age 11

"Charm, wit and even a bit of mystery. Honey Moon is a terrific piece of writing that will keep kids asking for more."
--Priscilla Strapp, Writer, Foster Mom

$14.99 US / $22.50 CAN

90000>

9 781943 785186

THE ENCHANTED WORLD OF

HONEY MOON

SHADES AND SHENANIGANS

Suzanne Brooks Kuhn   Created by Mark Andrew Poe

When Honey comes face-to-face with
Clarice Kligore and her Royal Shades
she knows something must be done to
keep this not very nice club from
taking over Sleepy Hollow Elementary.
Honey sets out to beat them at their
own game by forming her own club,
The Queen Bees. Instead of chasing the
Shades off the playground for good,
Honey learns that being the Queen Bee
is more about the honey than the sting.

"Honey goes where she is needed . . . and everyone needs Honey Moon!"
— David Kirkpatrick, Former Production Chief, Walt Disney Studios

"I wish Honey Moon had been written when
my girls were young. She would have charmed
her way into their hearts."
- Nora Wolfe, Mother of Two

"Heart, humor, age-
appropriate puppy love
and wisdom. Honey's
not perfect but she is
striving to be a good,
strong kid."
— Anne Brighen
Elementary School Teacher

"My favorite character of
all time. I love Honey."
- Elise Rogers, Age 9

"I am a grandmother. I knew ahead of time that these books were
aimed at younger readers but I could not resist and thank goodness
for that! A great kid's book!"
--Carri Zimmerman, Grandmother of Twelve

$14.99
ISBN 978-1-943785-16-2
51499>

THE ENCHANTED WORLD OF HONEY MOON

NOT YOUR VALENTINE

Regina Jennings   Created by Mark Andrew Poe

A Sleepy Hollow Valentine's Day dance with a boy! NO WAY, NO HOW is Honey Moon going to a scary sweetheart dance with that Noah kid. But, after being forced to dance together in PE class, word gets around that Honey likes Noah. Now, she has no choice but to stop Valentine's Day in its tracks. Things never go as planned and Honey winds up with the surprise of her Sleepy Hollow life.

"Honey is a breakout wonder... What a pint-sized powerhouse!"
- David Kirkpatrick, Former Production Chief, Walt Disney Studios

"A dance, a boy and Honey Moon - every girl wants to know how this story will end up."
- Deby Less, Mom and Teacher

"What better way to send a daughter off to sleep than knowing she can conquer any problem by doing the right thing."
- Jean Zyskowski Mom and Office Manager

"I love to read and Honey Moon is my favorite of all!"
- Lilah Black, KID age 8

"Makes me want to have daughters again so they could grow up with Honey Moon. Strong and vulnerable heroines make raising healthy children even more exciting.
-- Suzanne Kuhn, Best-selling Author Coach

$14.99
ISBN 978-1-943785-08-7
51499>

9 781943 785087